KENTUCKY SOLO

If Solomon Jackson had known what fate held in store before he abandoned his trap-lines and headed back to Kentucky, maybe he would never have set out. If curiosity had not tempted him, perhaps he would never have stumbled across Walter Krank and saved him from a miserable death. But then he would never have become a partner in a gold mine. Nor would he have found himself facing a gang of ruthless outlaws and a one-way ticket to Boot Hill!

Books by Ed Hunter
in the Linford Western Library:

BULLION MASSACRE
DOUBLE D SHOWDOWN
ELEPHANT GUN MALONE

C

ED HUNTER

◆

KENTUCKY SOLO

Complete and Unabridged

LINFORD
Leicester

First published in Great Britain in 1995 by
Robert Hale Limited
London

First Linford Edition
published 1998
by arrangement with
Robert Hale Limited
London

British Library CIP Data

Hunter, Ed
Kentucky Solo.—Large print ed.—
Linford western library
1. Western stories
2. Large type books
I. Title
823.9′14 [F]

ISBN 0–7089–5378–6

Published by
F. A. Thorpe (Publishing) Ltd.
Anstey, Leicestershire

Set by Words & Graphics Ltd.
Anstey, Leicestershire
Printed and bound in Great Britain by
T. J. International Ltd., Padstow, Cornwall

This book is printed on acid-free paper

1

Old Walter Krank sensed something was wrong. He had felt uneasy almost as soon as he broke camp and set off at daybreak to trudge across the many dusty ridges of the alkali plain. The hairs on the back of his neck kept on lifting at frequent intervals. Somewhere out there malevolent eyes were watching. Who they belonged to he did not know. He could not see them, but someone was there all right . . . following and waiting.

At the top of a ridge he stopped for a few moments and made a display of fanning himself with his battered wide-brimmed hat, at the same time wiping the dust and sweat from his face with his dirty white-spotted, red kerchief.

Tipping a ration of water from a canteen into his hat he held it for the animal to drink, then replaced the stetson's cooling wetness back on his head before quenching his own thirst. Afterwards he took his time checking and adjusting the ancient leather straps of the pannier frames on his grey-muzzled burro's back. Suddenly he heaved a sigh then spoke to her out of the side of his mouth as he chewed at the last of his wad.

'Well, somebody's out there. I just know it . . . and they ain't too friendly neither.' He slapped the animal's neck affectionately. 'Ya know, Gertrude,' he sighed, 'it's at times like these when I wish I'd invested in a good fast horse instead of a seven-dollar awkward cuss like you.'

Moving round to the other side of her, he noticed the black-tipped ears which stuck through the ragged-edged brim of the straw sombrero she wore. They twitched as though searching to locate a distant sound. Stretching her neck she bared her yellowed teeth and brayed loudly. Then she nudged him as though to confirm her understanding.

'Yeah, you know it as well as me.' He slapped her fondly on the other side of her thick neck then set about rearranging the load. Secretly, he made certain his Winchester was loose in its stowage, handy to reach, and ready cocked.

At every opportunity he peered from beneath half-closed eyelids, scanning the countryside for the slightest sign of movement, but without result.

'Could be Indians?' He spat then wiped his mouth with his sleeve. 'Or maybe I'm goin' loco,' he said out loud to himself, then shook his head. 'But I don't believe it . . . at least not about the Indians.'

Picking up the lead rope he turned his back on the burro and walked on. As the rope tightened he gave it a sharp tug.

'Gee-up! Gertrude, shift your lazy arse,' he advised. 'Before I fit my boot up it.'

They had reached the third ridge

when a rifle barked from behind cover and the lead rope jerked from the old-timer's hand. He distinctly heard the bullet thwack home. Turning, there was just time to watch helplessly as if caught up in the middle of some fantastic dream.

Gertrude snorted loudly, then went down on her knees. Coffee-pot and pans hanging on the panniers rattled and clanged. The burro's head flopped, crushing the ridiculous sombrero as she rolled on to her side. Short legs jerked and kicked wildly . . . but by reflex only.

★ ★ ★

Buzzards circled, black against the relentless glare of the afternoon sky. Solomon Jackson, mountain man, long unused to the torrid heat of the plains, reined his mount to a halt. Dragging down the sweat-soaked bandanna from his lower face he roughly wiped his brow on a well-worn buckskin shirt-sleeve. Then, shielding his half-closed blue eyes with cupped hands, he scanned across the sparse dried-out scrub and undulations of the alkali wilderness, into the shimmering haze.

'Well, Nelly, can't see nothin', but there's somethin' dead or dyin' over there,' he drawled at last. 'Satan's angels ain't flyin' around just t' pass the time of day.'

The sudden loudness of his words split the silence, startling a covey of desert quail which sprang from their dust bath, close by the side of the trail. He ignored them as they fled, their stubby wings frantically whirring through the oven-hot air.

'But man or beast,' he continued, shaking his head as he frowned. 'I sure as hell don't know which.'

His long-legged riding mule left one enormously long ear pointing after the retreating quail, the other she flicked back and directed at her master. Tossing her head, she jingled her silver-trimmed bridle and snorted as if in response. Solomon grinned, leaned forward and smacked the side of her neck with several hard, but fond slaps.

'Yeah, I reckon you an' me, we're of the same mind.' With an almost imperceptible movement of his weathered hands, he neck-reined Nelly around to the new direction, then nudged her into an ungainly, deceptively fast canter. 'Let's go see.'

In places the alkali gave way to ragged patches of mesquite and sagebrush growing around wind-smoothed rocks and shale. But it made little difference. The big white mule moved as confidently as a fine lady strolling across her own fancy drawing-room. Only when Solomon sat back in the saddle did she check her pace and slow to a walk again.

A fat old burro wearing a straw hat and with denuded pannier frames still strapped on its back, lay on its side beside a slab of rock. Dead, the animal's belly was already swollen with putrefaction gasses and its short legs stuck out, straight and stiff like those of an ugly carved table. Around its genitals and head openings, heaving swarms of noisy blowflies went industriously about their business.

Behind the rock and only a few feet further on, a man naked to the waist, was pegged out like a drying buffalo hide. From the sides of his head, tufts of white hair was plastered stiff with coagulated blood, while from his age-wrinkled brow backwards, more flies had gathered to feast on a wide strip of red-raw skull.

'Jesus . . . scalped!' Solomon slipped from the saddle and, grabbing one of his canteens, hurried to kneel by the man's side. 'Hey, old-timer. You still livin'?' he asked as he testily waved the flies from the bloody scalp and splashed water on to the sunburned and cracked lips.

Slowly, with great difficulty the man responded. First the pink tip of a tobacco-stained tongue curled from his mouth and licked along the lips, savouring the life-saving moisture. After half a dozen such sips he displayed signs of further and stronger recovery. Cracking first one eye open, then the other, he looked up at Solomon, and cleared his throat noisily, before emitting a series of dried croaks.

'Bastards . . . bushwhackers. They robbed me.'

'Yeah, I'd already figured that much on my ownsome. Now lie still old-timer, and I'll cut you loose.' Slipping a massive hunting knife from its sheath, Solomon snicked easily through the dried-out rawhide then attempted to move the old-timer to the shade of a rock.

'Aah! Christ almighty, you tryin' t' kill me, young fella?'

'Sorry, Pop, what's your trouble?'

'Ya mean, apart from the lead slug them varmints left in my back, that and a busted leg?'

'Like I said, sorry, I didn't know.'

'Well you take my word for it, I'm a-tellin' ya, ain't I?' the old-timer snapped. Then he softened. 'Say, son, you don't happen to have a drink handy, do ya?'

Solomon ignored the request.

'Who did this?' he asked instead.

'Well it weren't no friends,' the reply was growled back. 'That's for damned sure.' Lowering his voice as suddenly as it had been raised, he persisted. 'Hey, fella, ya never answered me, about that drink.'

The mountain man unplugged the stopper from the neck of the canteen before handing it to him. The old man shook it a little, sniffed at it, then with an intense look of distaste stared at his rescuer.

'Water!' He sighed heavily. 'You're a hard man, Mister . . . er, what's yer name?'

'Solomon Jackson,' the other offered. 'But mostly folks find it easier t' call me Solo.' Pointing to the stranger's

9

right leg he asked, 'This the one that's busted?'

'Uh-huh, can't ya tell?'

Solo looked pointedly at the other man, but said nothing. Running his knife blade along the seam, he slit the dirt-encrusted trouser leg from the ankle to the hip.

'And you, Pop, what's your handle, eh?'

'Krank's the name. Walter Krank.' For a short spell he studied Solo. 'Seein' as how ya cut me loose, I guess you can call me Walt.' Suddenly he smiled. 'Hey, that's a good idea. We can drink on that.'

'Maybe, Walt,' Solo grinned broadly, displaying strong white teeth. 'After I've fixed up this leg o' yours.'

Walt's wrinkled face showed disappointment, then twisted with acute pain as Solo began to manipulate the broken limb.

'Yep, you're right. This leg's good an' broke,' he informed the sweating patient. 'Just you lay there an' keep

10

still while I rustle up some splints to hold it t'gether.'

'Keep still?' Walt exploded. 'Ya thinkin' I'll be climbin' into my Sunday best an' dashin' away to some hoedown?' Abruptly he changed tack again. 'This leg o' mine hurts awful bad, boy. A good slug o' whisky would sure help a man of my age to bear up. I just know it would.'

Within minutes Solo returned with some lengths of wood cut from the pannier frame of the dead burro. Dangling from his index finger was a heavy-glazed earthenware jug. Walt's eyes brightened as he wiped at his mouth with the back of his hand.

'Whisky!'

'Uh-huh . . . mountain-style. The real stuff, made it myself.'

'It's been a coon's age since I had me some of that,' Walt smacked his lips noisily as he was passed the jug.

'Well, you'd better take a decent swig, then I can get started an' work

11

on this leg of yours.'

Setting the bones in Walt's leg turned out to be quite straightforward. Apart from a lot of loud cursing and yelling from Walt, the break was soon dealt with.

Bandaging the scalped head presented no real problem either, except for another tirade of swearing. It was the hunk of lead still lodged in the cantankerous old man's back which promised to be the real trouble.

'It's in real deep, Pop. I don't know enough for that. I'd have to poke about to find it. You need a proper sawbones, a fella who knows what he's doin',' Solo advised. 'I could end up killin' you.'

'Hell, boy, of course ya could kill me. I know that.' Walt smiled. 'But there ain't no doc . . . not within the Lord knows how many miles of here. If that bullet stays in, the wound'll go bad. I'll die anyhow.' Adjusting his position, he gasped. 'The way I see it, like it or not, you bought in to this

12

hand. How ya bet in the game . . . well, it's all up t' you.'

'I've fixed broken bones, done some stitchin', made a poultice or two. I can even mix herbs like the Indians showed me.' Solo frowned, shook his head and grimaced. 'But I ain't never dug a bullet out of man nor beast . . . not in all my life.'

'Take it easy, son.' Walt smiled again. 'Now, why don't ya have a slug from that friendly old jug and . . . ' — he winked — 'pour me another four or five fingers more in that coffee mug, to settle this dang-awful pain, before ya go in for real with that knife.'

★ ★ ★

To Solo, it seemed at first as though the old-timer would turn up his toes and die, but he was far tougher than he looked and clung to life like he intended to live for ever. Solo sat beside him in the blanket shelter he had rigged, dutifully staying awake just in case.

It was close to sunrise. The distant coyotes had ceased their mournful howling, and the purple sky was changing to a line of warm yellow tongues with splashes of orange on the eastern horizon. Walt was still fast asleep, and snoring noisily at regular intervals.

Ruefully, Solo wished he was doing the same. He shivered, rubbed his hands together, then yawned and stretched powerful arms as he got stiffly to his feet. Quietly, not wanting to awaken the old-timer, he crossed to the camp-fire and, after raking the embers back into flame, added more fuel. The night had been long and wearisome. He reckoned he had earned and deserved a good breakfast.

The thickly-sliced salt bacon spluttered noisily in the smoke-blackened skillet. Its smell coupled with the rich aroma of fresh coffee caused his mouth to water in eager anticipation.

'Hey, Solo,' a voice called from the makeshift shelter. 'I like my coffee good an' strong, and my bacon needs t' be sliced nice an' thick, and only a mite underdone.'

For a moment a surge of anger coursed through the mountain man, and then he saw the funny side. Keeping his back to the shelter, Solo grinned.

'Oh, so you ain't dead yet?' he yelled back. 'As for breakfast . . . didn't cook you none. Reckoned if you're gonna die there ain't no point in wastin' good grub.'

Even as he spoke he tilted the frying pan and tipped the bacon on to a ready-warmed tin plate, then poured a mug of coffee.

'Now shut yer noise. Get this down your scrawny neck, and give me some peace will ya?' Solo grumbled, concealing his grin as he went and handed the drink and grub to the old-timer. 'Else I'm goin' to starve to death.'

'Hey, you'll have to prop me up. A fella can't eat his vittles an' drink, not when he's lyin' flat on his back, can he?'

'I knew it. I just knew you was goin' to be trouble the minute I laid eyes on ya.' Solo moved his own saddle over to support Walt in a sitting position. 'Anythin' else?'

'Sure . . . I've an itch that's worryin' my back somethin' awful,' the old man smirked. 'It needs a real good scratchin'.'

'And you . . . can kiss my arse,' the mountain man grunted, stomping out to tend to the urgent needs of his own belly. Once out of earshot, he grinned. 'Tough old buzzard.'

* * *

On the fifth day after the makeshift operation, they agreed that the bullet wound was not healing as fast as they had hoped. However, the initial swelling of the broken leg had subsided, and much of the pain had gone.

The two men each of whom, by choice, had lived as loners for years, had, in the short time since they'd been thrown together, grown to respect and even like one another.

'Ya never said why ya left the mountains to travel down through this part of the country?' Walt pressed as the younger man returned from a scouting expedition, dragging two larch saplings behind Nelly. 'Did ya?'

'Felt like a change.' Using the straps from the dead burro's broken pannier frames, Solo prepared a travois and secured one end on his white mule's back.

'So, where were ya headin', Solo?'

'Kentucky. The place I was born.'

'You got kinfolk there, son?'

'Nope. They've all passed on.'

Walter Krank, almost lost in the oversize buckskin shirt Solo had given him, twisted his bandaged head to one side and squinted out of one eye.

'Oh . . . a woman then?'

Solomon spread a blanket over the frame and tied it securely before he went on to explain.

'Had me some moments, but didn't want t' be hogtied too soon.'

'Well, the way I sees it, there ain't no point in ya goin'. You've been before, so you already know what's there.' He waited for an argument but when none came, he continued. 'Ya know, you an' me, we'd make a good twosome.'

Solo's eyebrows arched high.

'Oh yeah, doin' what?'

'Prospectin' . . . what else? I tell ya, son, it was your lucky day when you ran into me. Do yourself a favour.' He tapped at the side of his bulbous nose. 'This's as good as any bird-dog. I've got a real nose for gold, son.'

Solo shook his head emphatically.

'No. I ain't no miner, and I don't aim to live like no gopher in a hole in the ground.'

Walt pretended he had not beard Solo's objections.

'You got any money?'

Solo paused, then carried on securing the bedding on the travois, ready for the journey.

'Some . . . why?'

'Aw heck, ya know I've been robbed.'

'So?' Solo shrugged. His voice had a hard edge to it. 'I didn't rob you, did I?'

'No. Never said ya did.' Hesitant, Walt wiped his mouth again. 'But I'll be needin' me a grubstake.' Growing more confident he perked up. 'Yes sir, I'll cut ya in, a straight fifty-fifty partnership. Right down the line. All proper and legal, on paper like it should be.'

'Thanks, but no thanks, Walt. I've told you, I never did take a shine t' diggin'. And the thoughts of being in a hole, with all that rock an' dirt just a few feet above waitin' t' bury me, gives me the shiverin' willies.'

Manoeuvring Nelly so that the travois was drawn up next to the prospector, he explained further. 'Besides all that, I had to work damned hard for my money. Had me some real lean years, in all kinds of weather. Ask anyone who knows, and it's likely they'll tell ya, it ain't easy, just stayin' alive, tappin' fur in the high country.'

The prospector tut-tutted and let out a heavy sigh showing a mixture of disgust and disappointment.

'Do ya always dang-well go off at half-cock?' Walt asked acidly as the younger man gave him a helping hand to transfer then settle himself onto the travois. 'First of all, who in tarnation mentioned any diggin'? I sure as hell didn't, so ya won't have to go scratchin' a livin' in no hole. Secondly . . . I've already found me a good claim, producin' real quality colour, and it's all legalized an' properly registered at the government office.'

Solo's only reaction to this news was to ask an obvious and cautious question.

'Then why d' you need my money, eh?'

'Because I was friggin'-well robbed,

20

wasn't I?' the old-timer shouted in frustration. 'Sweet Jesus, you blind or somethin'?' Angered he made an attempt to sit up on the travois, but Solo reached out and easily pushed him back down then secured him with a rope as the old man ranted on.

'The no-account varmints who did the bushwhackin' and staked me out, took my three pokes of top-grade dust.'

'Dust?'

'Yeah . . . gold dust, along with some real nice nuggets. Totallin' close on two thousand dollars' worth, maybe more. They wanted me to tell 'em where my claim certificate was. I wouldn't say. That's why the bastards scalped me and smashed my leg with a rock. The low-down skunks even shot my old mule . . . smashed my shovel an' every damn thing. And ya saw how they left me. Hell, Solo, now I ain't nothin' but an old, worn-out, no-account hobo.'

'Sure, but at least you're still a livin' one,' the mountain man pointed out dryly. 'How far is it to the next town?

Did you say thirty miles, eh?'

'Uh-huh, but on second thoughts, forty could be nearer the mark. But no more than ten to a water-hole.'

Solo, used to moving out from temporary campsites, checked around as he always did, to see that nothing of importance had been forgotten.

'Well,' he said finally, sticking the haft of his hand-axe through the loop in his belt, as if to balance the heavyweight hunting knife sheathed on his right hip. 'There ain't no point in us lingerin' on here, is there? You ready?'

'Uh-huh, what ya waitin' for?'

Solomon Jackson clicked his tongue and the big mule leaned forward and began to drag the load with ease.

For a while the prospector studied the mountain man striding alongside the travois in silence.

'Good mule that,' Walt commented. 'Not often you see a white one. Albino, is it?'

'Nope. Look at her eyes, they're black as coal, and the sun don't bother

her none, not like an albino.'

'Where'd ya get her?'

'Turkey shoot four years back. Nelly
. . . she was first prize, I could've sold
her a dozen times over, there an' then,
but I'd taken a shine to her. Yes, sir,
that was the best day's work I ever did,
winnin' her.'

'You get that fancy Mexican saddle
an' bridle with her?'

'Hell, no, got that at another turkey
shoot, two years later.'

'Mmm.' Wald sounded thoughtful.
'Turkey shoots . . . seems you can
handle a gun then?'

'Yeah . . . some.'

'Ain't seen ya wear no gunbelt.'

'Don't have one. Never had the
need. Only use a rifle or a hand gun
to fill my belly, or win me a few dollars
in competitions.'

'And what kind of guns d' ya
favour?' Walt's curiosity was growing.
'A Colt . . . a Winchester, a Henry, or
what?'

'No. Nothin' so fancy,' Solo admitted.

'When I was a kid, before I left home, my pa gave me a Kentucky long-rifle an' matchin' pistol . . . showed me how to use 'em. They've been all I've ever needed.'

'A Kentucky? Jumpin' jack-rabbits!' Walt gaped in disbelief. 'Ya mean, ya still use . . . flintlocks?'

'Sure. Why not? They do the job.'

'Come on,' Walt scoffed. 'Even redskins don't use single-shot muzzle-loaders these days, not unless they've had 'em to a gunsmith's, gettin' converted to take nipple-caps.'

'Well I like 'em,' Solo countered. 'Powder and lead are cheap. But them fancy, ready-made brass-cased cartridges cost a whole heap more.'

'Yeah, there ain't no denyin' that,' the prospector agreed. 'There's a lot o' sense in that.' Then he prepared to play his ace. 'But tell me, Solo,' he leered craftily, 'what would ya do if you're in a saloon one day, mindin' your own business, when three fellas on the prod, stroll in?'

24

'Three fellas?' Solo considered. 'What about 'em?'

'They don't like you mountain men . . . so they decide to have fun and call ya out. And there you are, you're standin' out in the street, up to yer ankles in horse-shit, with two old guns . . . and only one shot loaded in each.'

Walt sniggered as he asked his final question. 'Tell me . . . what d' you thing would happen, eh?'

Solomon Jackson kept looking ahead, his stride never faltering. Without so much as a frown, or any need to ponder on the question, he answered confidently in his quiet southern drawl, 'There'd be three dead men.'

2

To the normally lonesome Solomon Jackson, it seemed every few yards along the road into town, groups of curious people were gathered. Sophisticated townsfolk, dressed in the latest fashions imported directly from the mail-order houses in St Louis, pointed derisive fingers, while others sniggered, apparently making fun of the newcomers.

Solo gritted his teeth.

'Maybe we should've sold tickets,' he growled.

The day was a hot one. Women sheltered behind fluttering Chinese fans or cheap paper parasols. Young and not so young lustfully eyed the big mountain man who strode past them with such easy grace alongside the white mule. Automatically they compared his wild, buckskin-clad muscular frame and majestic bearing, to the fat or weedy statures and pompous gaits of their own pampered men.

Their slick go-getting spouses were already thinking along the lines of profit and loss. Each was fully aware that whenever strangers hit town, fortune could change, especially if they turned out to be different. In their conservative world of business, different meant dangerous!

Solo pulled up Nelly. He strolled over to the nearside of the road and selected a white-aproned store clerk busy sweeping the boardwalk outside a general store.

'Say, fella, has this here town got a doctor?'

The sweeper looked up but before he could answer, a bystander butted in.

'Sure has . . . two of 'em,' the townie exclaimed more than a little boastfully. But almost as quickly he leaned his head forward, bird-like, his beady eyes oozing suspicion as they fixed upon Solo's. 'Why, mister? What you want a doctor for? You ain't brought in anythin' catchin', like the smallpox, or maybe the plague, have you?'

Solo stared. The inquisitive man backed slowly and the remaining blood drained quickly from his already unhealthy pallid features. Realizing he had made a bad mistake, he forced a smile.

'Naw,' he whined. 'I was jokin'. Anyone can tell you ain't man like that.' Still keeping his eyes on Solo, he pointed further along the street. 'Go to Doc Gruber . . . little foreign fella, but a good doctor. You'll see his plate on the door. The other fella's further along. He's more a veterinary.'

'Thanks,' Solo muttered grudgingly. Then he returned to move the mule on again.

'Solo?'

'Yeah, Walt, what is it?'

'See that pinto in that yard over there?'

Solo turned his head and located the animal standing quietly among others in a fenced yard at the side of a livery.

'Yeah, I see it. What of it?'

'That horse belongs to one of the bushwhackers. The same fella who smashed my leg with the rock.'

'You sure?'

'Think I'm blind? You're damned right I'm sure.'

'All right . . . keep your hair on,' Solo answered, then had to stifle a grin as he suddenly realized what he had said. But if the old-timer had noticed the unintentional quip, he made no comment.

'Well, Solo . . . what ya goin' to do about it?'

'Me? Nothin',' Solomon stated casually, but with finality in his tone. 'I'm just bent on gettin' you to a sawbones like I said.'

'But what about the guy who broke my leg?'

'There'll be time enough to sort him out later,' was all he would be drawn to say. Guiding the mule to the left Solo halted it outside a neat clapboard house with clean curtains at its sparkling windows. He read the gleaming brass name-plate screwed to the front door. 'This is it.'

Having left the cantankerous old-timer in the capable hands of the medical man, Solomon made his way to the livery stable yard. He hung around for a while but nothing happened. Then a spotty-faced, over-fed youth came into the yard with a generous forkful of hay to put in the feed rack. Solo strolled closer to the fence and waved to the youngster. Suspiciously the boy approached half-way towards him, holding the now empty hayfork on guard as though it was a rifle.

'You want somethin', mister?'

'Yeah . . . that horse.' Solo pointed to the pinto now pulling at the hay with the other animals. 'Who does that belong to?'

'Why . . . ya wanna buy it?'. The youth ambled closer, interested.

'Maybe.'

'My old man owns it, along with

all the rest. He owns the whole dang shootin' match, and it'll be all mine when he snuffs it.' He waved his arm to demonstrate. 'The stables, the barn, the yard . . . an' everythin' in 'em.'

'Lucky you,' Solo drawled. 'How long's your pa owned it . . . the pinto?'

'Three days.' Holding the fork vertical and placing the handle on the ground he leaned on it with one hand while he thoughtfully scratched the tops off a couple of spots. 'Well, you interested or not?'

'What was he like . . . the fella your pa did the deal with? Was he on his own, or what?' He waited while the youth deliberated what to do. 'Well?'

'There were three of 'em. He was big, like you. But kind of stupid, if ya know what I mean?'

'Stupid?'

'Yeah, all mouth. Thought he knew everythin'. Said he wanted t'buy the best horse Pa had in the stables.' He sniggered. 'Never even had the sense to bid. Paid more'n twice what anyone else would've. Yeah,' he smirked. 'And in gold, too.'

'Coin?' Solo raised his eyebrows.

'No, dust.'

'He was a prospector?'

'Ha!' The youth laughed in disgust. 'Leastways that's what he said he was. All three of 'em did. But they sure didn't look like no prospectors t' me. To my mind, they were more like saddle tramps. Exceptin' they had guns . . . yeah, plenty of guns.'

'The horse your pa sold. What did it look like?' Solo pressed.

'A stallion. Big, an' black as pitch all over 'ceptin' for the white socks on its back legs and its nearside fore. Oh yeah, and it had a twisted star on its forehead.'

Solomon took a dollar from his pants pocket and the lad was drawn like a horse to sugar. His avaricious gaze fixed on the coin; he even forgot to scratch his spots.

'Did ya happen to hear anythin' them fellas said among themselves?

32

Like their names maybe, or where they were headin' next?' His agile fingers twirled the coin. 'Anythin', anythin' at all?'

'One of 'em, was always breakin' wind, worse than a horse let out on new spring grass. And the one they called Squint, on account of his queer eye . . . he laughed like a fool jackass when he mentioned they'd have t' go back to the diggin's for a refill.'

'The diggin's? Any idea where they might be?'

'Not me, mister, I know about hay an' corn an' horse-shit. Stable work, that's all.'

'I'll be around town for a while.' Solomon tossed the dollar to the youth who deftly caught it in his grimy fist. 'If you think of anything else I should know, seek me out.'

★ ★ ★

Walter Krank had stayed under the doctor's roof for more than three weeks before he was pronounced fit enough to leave. Solomon paid the bill without protest and bought a suitable outfit of clothes and boots for the old prospector from a mercantile. After that, he took him along to the livery stable to buy a horse.

'You ain't gonna be leavin' me now,' Walter exclaimed in surprise after Solo had folded the bill of sale and given it to him. 'Not when I really need ya?'

'What ya need me for?' the mountain man chided. 'I ain't yer momma.' Deliberately he gathered the reins in his hand and prepared to mount up on Nelly who, already loaded with his bedroll and saddle-bags, chomped noisily at her bit.

'Ya know damned well what for. To get even with the bushwhackers who robbed me. You ain't forgotten, have ya? Hell, son, when I was all pegged out and nearly dyin' back there, you practically promised in blood.'

'Whoa . . . now just you hold it right there, old timer.' Dropping the reins he let them dangle. 'I did no such thing. I never ever make a promise unless I intend to see it through to the bitter end.' He stabbed his forefinger at Walter. 'An' you know darned well, I made no such promise . . . to you, or anyone else.'

With a petulant display, Walter dragged the bill of sale back out of his pocket, crumpled it then stuffed it under the white mule's headband.

'Here, mister, you can keep your damned charity. I don't need a horse from no . . . Indian-giver.' With his shoulders hunched, he thrust a thumb into the belt of his new pants. Leaning heavily on his crutch, he then limped away, the toe of his trailing boot kicking up the dust from the street.

He had barely reached halfway across when Solo's enormous hand closed on his shoulder and twisted him round.

'Wait . . . ya cantankerous old coot. Ya gone loco or somethin', eh?'

Walter's lips compressed into a tight downward curving line of determination.

He started furiously into the laughing face of his benefactor, but stayed silent.

'Come on, let's you an' me go see the sheriff, eh?' Solo pulled gently and the old man didn't resist. 'Maybe he's heard somethin' since I first called in to see him.'

'Sheriff? Huh!' Walter spat into the dust. He pointed at the gob of spit as it slowly soaked into the dust. 'The sheriff of this town's not worth that much. He ain't a real sheriff . . . just one o' them politicals who didn't earn the job like most lawmen do. He just got himself elected into it.' Walt spat again. 'I know. I heard the doc' sayin' it to his missus. And remember, the doc's an educated man . . . so he should know.'

Walter was right. Apart from entering reported crime into his book, the town's lawman had done nothing.

'So, you're just goin' t' sit there, polishin' that chair with yer big fat arse while them outlaws live it up on my money?' a disgusted Walter exclaimed.

'Mister, if you're takin' wages for this job then you're a bigger damned robber than any of 'em.'

'Listen t' me . . . old man,' the sheriff sneered. 'Your kind don't pay to local taxes towards my wages, so don't you come in here shootin' off your mouth. If you were younger, I'd give ya a good lickin' an' let ya cool off in them cells back there, for sassin' an officer of the law.'

'Ha! Law? Hell, boy, I bet ya can't even spell the word. And as for lickin' . . . folks round these parts all know what sort of lickin' ya did t' get your job.' Walt rounded on his heel and spoke to Solo. 'We'll have t' forget the law in this town.' He thumbed over his shoulder at the scarlet-faced sheriff. 'That bastard has.'

The mountain man had stood there, arms folded across his chest, leaning his back against the office wall, doing and saying nothing. He laughed as Walter, still mouthing-off, limped determinedly past him.

'Hey, hold on. Just one cotton-pickin' minute, you ornery old goat.' Shooting a sideways look of disdain at the sheriff, he strode after the loudly-cursing prospector, whose anger had driven him quickly on in spite of his game leg and cumbersome wooden crutch.

'Told ya it would be a complete waste of time, didn't I . . . eh?'

'Yeah, so ya did, Walt,' Solo admitted, catching up with his friend. 'Cool down a mite. Let's find us some shade and share a bottle while we think on things.'

Walter's anger subsided, evaporating like dew under the rays of the rising sun. He smiled.

'That's the first sensible notion you've come up with all day.'

Sitting in a shady corner of the main saloon of the Golden Garter, they argued the best part of a bottle of whisky away.

'Ya owe me, Solo,' Walter jabbered.

'Nuts!'

'Nuts?' Walter frowned, bemused.

'Ya went an' saved my hide, didn't ya?'

'So?'

'Well, then. That makes ya kinda responsible. If you'd let me die, I'd not be in this situation I'm in now.' The prospector tapped his nose secretively as he gawped, red-eyed with booze, around the sparse sprinkling of customers. With great difficulty he crooked his finger and thumb close, almost touching together and held them in front of Solo's nose. 'You and me . . . we're just that far away from bein' stinkin' rich. Yes sir, just that far.' Leaning closer he whispered, 'Come 'ere. No, don't laugh, fella, I'm serious.'

'OK, Pop,' Solo chuckled. He sucked in his cheeks and stopped grinning. 'What ya want to say, eh?'

'Yer gonna be a real pal. Yer gonna grub-stake me, ain't ya?' He pushed his face closer still. 'Partners. You an' me . . . even shares, right down the line.' He hooked his sinewy arm around Solo's neck and breathed whisky fumes

39

all over him. 'What ya say . . . eh?'

Solo started at the intent multi-wrinkled features. The old man was rough and tough, but there was no doubt in his mind that Walter was honest.

'All right,' Solo sighed at last. 'If that'll get your arm from around my neck and stop ya chokin' me with whisky fumes, yeah, I'll stake ya. Now, tell me . . . partner . . . what'll we need?'

'Another bottle to celebrate,' was the instant and delighted reply. 'But make it the good stuff. You an' me are goin' to make a night of it. We'll wait till mornin'. Then we'll do the business end proper and list things down on paper.'

★ ★ ★

In spite of not wanting a partnership; especially an active one, Solomon Jackson found himself heading back along the same trail again. Beside

40

him a jubilant Walter Krank straddled a chestnut gelding and urged on a couple of lop-eared burros laden with prospecting equipment and gunny sacks stuffed with food supplies.

'Ya, ain't never gonna look back an' regret this deal we done, Solo.'

'You're too late, old-timer,' the mountain man muttered laconically to himself. 'I already do.'

For a dozen days more they travelled on, during which time each man held his own counsel, saying only what needed to be said. Not until they had left behind the arid plains and arrived at some foothills, did the old man perk up and become talkative again, even singing at times.

'How far now?' Solo asked, attempting to prevent yet another monotonous song droned in a tuneless fashion. They were traversing fertile country, criss-crossed with streams and meandering rivers which over the centuries had eroded deep gorges through the rock.

'Only another day or so.'

'That's what ya told me near on a week ago.'

Solo's partner grinned.

'That's a slight failin' of mine, son. Ya see, I've lived without a clock so long I never did get the hang of botherin' about time. Spring, winter, summer an' fall, that's all that concerns me.'

Three days later they arrived at the bank of a clear, gravel-bedded river.

'Nearly there,' Walt mentioned. Without further explanation he turned along its bank to follow the river upstream. Here, virgin pine woods grew right down to the water's edge. In places the tougher going was almost impassable for the pack-animals. But Walt, old as he was, was well used to it and took it all in his stride, the same as the younger man.

Together, using the blades of their new shovels like scythes, they worked side by side, slashing a passage through the undergrowth for themselves and their animals.

Further along, the bank merged with the side of a towering cliff which jutted out into the river, forcing them to take to the shallows and wade around the obstructions. The water, fresh from the mountains up ahead, was ice-cool and because of the narrowing of the waterway, flowed much faster than it had downstream.

'Any time now,' Walt shouted above the noise generated by the water cascading over the rocks.

Upstream above the gorge the river widened out. Here its waters ran slower and more tranquil again. Another jutting cliff face forced them on to the edge of the river bank again, causing them to pick their path over well-worn rock and around the bulbous spur of equally smooth granite.

With this obstruction safely negotiated, Solomon Jackson reined Nelly to a halt and stood in the stirrups, peering out over an elder bush.

Before him, a less densely wooded valley opened out. Set back from the river bank, he saw a single-roomed cabin in a clearing. At the far end of the clearing a privy stood alone. At the near side of the cabin was a log pile and beside it, a chopping block with a rusting felling axe stuck in it.

'Who lives there, Walt?'

'Me . . . me an' you,' Walter answered proudly. 'That's our place.' He rode up closer, stopped, and parted the branches of the elder with his hands. He grimaced as he peered through the gap. 'It's our place, but somebody else has been tryin' it out for a while.'

'How d' ya know?'

'Whenever I go away for a time, I always make sure all the unsplit logs on the top of the woodpile are in line. I've always done it. That way I know if anybody's been stayin' when they ain't supposed to.' He nodded at the woodpile. 'Look at them logs. Some's been used since I've been gone. And the axe, I'd never leave it out there in the open to rust.'

'Well, there ain't no smoke comin'

from the chimney now,' Solo pointed out. 'But still, we might as well show a lick of sense and be cautious. It won't hurt none to check around.' Slipping quietly from his saddle he took his long-barrelled pistol from the nearside saddle-bag and checked the pan was charged with powder. Satisfied, he cocked the serpentine hammer and was all set for action.

'I'll come with ya,' Walter said, dismounting then reaching to unhook his crutch from the pannier cradle of the leading burro.

'No. You stay undercover and whistle if ya lay eyes on anyone,' Solo insisted. Then, silent as a hunting cat, he slipped into the greenery and in seconds was gone from sight.

A little later on, Solo emerged confidently from the far side of the cabin, eased the hammer off-cock and slipped the pistol into the front of his pants belt.

'We're on our own, Walt. Come on in, I think you'll know who's been here.' He hunkered down and pointed to some clear prints in the moist earth. 'What ya think? Anyone ya know?'

'Yeah . . . it was them,' Walt stated emphatically. 'I tell ya, I'd know them square-toed bootprints anywhere. Them varmints must've found this place after I left for town, stayed the night, then trailed me down to the plain.'

'Well, I'd never have found ya,' Solo pointed out, 'if they'd come earlier and caught ya here.'

Walter mused, removing his hat and cautiously fingering his healing scalp.

'Maybe if them murderin' varmints had done that they would've taken more than a couple of pokes of dust and my hair.'

* * *

Solo had got the fire going in the hearth and the coffee-pot bubbling, when Walter handed him a crumpled newspaper.

'Look what I found in the privy.

Take a look at the date,' he advised.

Solo inspected the news-sheet but did not answer right away.

'Hmm!' He rested his chin in his cupped hand. 'It's from that newspaper office in that town we just left. And printed long before we set off for here.'

'It sure was,' his partner snarled. 'The same darned day you took me in there on that travois. I remember because that doc had a fancy calendar hangin' next t' my bed. Them bushwhackin' bastards, they've been back here again since then . . . just like they own the place.'

'Well, that may be so; I'll check around again, but you can't do anythin', except forget 'em. They ain't likely to come back, but if they do, we'll have our eyes open and be ready for 'em. Meanwhile, we'll hang around here, do some pannin' and tidy this place up good enough for decent folks t' live in.'

'Who says? And What's wrong with the place, eh?'

'Me . . . I say.' Solo waved his hand at the interior of the shack and wrinkled his nose. 'I ain't livin' in it. Not while it stinks like a pig-farmer's old boots.'

'Well . . . it could do with a woman's touch,' Walter conceded grudgingly, swiftly changing the subject when he realized that his words were falling on deaf ears. He made one more play. 'Supposin' them murderers come back . . . I might not be so lucky next time.'

3

The following month passed quickly. From sun-up to sunset the two of them worked stripped to the waist under the relentless heat of the sun. Each day, Solo felled timber while Walt used the burros with drag chains to transport the lumber to the claim.

Together they split the tree trunks into rough planks by means of hammers and wedges, then constructed a new and much bigger rocker-box, able to hold more gravel. To improve their output further, they built a sluice to carry water from a small waterfall to separate the gold dust from the dirt.

Almost without him realizing, Walt's injuries healed and his memories of the bushwhackers faded to the back of his mind.

To his surprise, Solo found himself infected by the excitement of finding gold and watching their horde of the heavy precious metal build up. He began to realize that soon he would be able to buy what he liked, or go anywhere he wanted, and do almost anything he pleased.

'Ya surely didn't lie t' me when you said you'd found a good claim,' Solo stated one evening as he tipped the pan of the table scales to fill another leather poke. 'You an' me, we're doin' real good, Walt.'

Walter hefted the filled sack in the palm of his hand then winked across the table to his partner.

'Son, ya don't know the half of it. If everythin' works out, another year like this and we'll have earned enough to set up properly and hire us a crew of miners.' He grinned and got up, then walked about using his hands expressively to substantiate his words. 'T' my way of thinkin', the mother-lode's not far away. Once we've a proper mine sunk into that cliff, we'll be into big money. Mark my words.

We'll be wearin' dude suits . . . smokin' two-dollar cigars, and takin' a bath in twelve-year-old malt whisky.'

'Ya practically do that now,' Solo put in. 'The whisky bit, I mean.'

Walt didn't bite. Instead he mischievously winked again and leered. 'And we'll have a proper house . . . with one o' them real big bendin' staircases. Ya know what I mean, where rich folks like us can entertain more high-kickin' women than a top-rate whorehouse.'

'I thought you couldn't abide women?'

'I do when I can afford 'em . . . but I like t' treat 'em real good.'

Solo lifted the whisky jug, shook it and tipped it upside-down. He pursed his lips as, slowly, a single drop dripped from the neck and splashed on to the table top.

'I guess ya can forget havin' a bath in booze . . . ' he said. 'Right now I'd settle for enough to fill a glass.'

The happiness in Walt's face abruptly died. In disbelief he picked up the empty jug and peered inside.

'It can't be. Don't tell me that's the last jug?'

'Told ya last week you were goin' at it too hard,' Solo grumbled. 'But ya paid no heed, ya still went at it like we had a whole lake full of the stuff.'

'Well keep yer hair on. It ain't exactly a serious case o' life or death, is it? We can easily get more.'

'Oh yeah?' Doubt was evident in Solo's voice.

'Yeah! That's what I said. We'll go get some t'morro', eh?'

'Where?'

Walt winked, and tapped his nose as usual.

'You'll find out.'

* * *

Solo and Walt set out a little after sunrise next day. All morning they travelled upstream, glad to be in the saddle again instead of bent over the rocker box or shovelling gravel.

'You'll like old Henry, and he'll be mighty glad to meet ya,' Walter prophesied, shouting above the noise of the river cascading over the rocks.

'Who's Henry?' Solomon yelled back. He had never heard mention of the man until that moment.

'Henry? He staked a claim further up-river, just a month or so after me. Lives on his ownsome,' his partner explained. 'His claim ain't much good but he makes the best damned moonshine a body ever tasted.'

As soon as Solo spotted Henry he saw at a glance the old recluse would not be distilling any more moonshine. The ingeniously improvised still was standing there for all to see, under a lean-to roof to shelter it from the weather. But its coil of copper condenser-tubing had turned green and there was no smoke from the chimney. Its fire had gone out . . . just like Henry's.

Henry stood silent and alone. His limbs had been forced out straight, and spread to form a diagonal cross. Someone had nailed him against the wall of his own log cabin, and had used six-inch long spikes to do it.

Even as the mounts splashed out of the river shallows and struggled up on to the bank, Solo could see Walt's old pal had had his stomach slit open. His guts had spilled out and hung like tangled snakes. Someone had used a knife lower down so that the moonshiner could no longer claim to be a man.

'Good God,' Walter was finally able to exclaim as they approached his old pal. 'He's been crucified,' he added unnecessarily.

Within spitting distance of the corpse, they could not help but recoil at the sickly-sweet stench of death. Flies swirled up in a black cloud. Angrily, Walt snatched off his hat and waved it furiously at the mass of insects still clustered on his dead friend's head and face. The blowflies hummed up like angry bees and revealed that Henry had also been scalped . . . in the same manner as Walter.

Shocked, Walter leaned against the log wall and stood looking down at his feet and shaking his head. After a series of heavy sobs had racked his body, he sniffed, then turned a sorrowful twisted face to Solomon.

'It's them, Solo. Just take a gander at that style o' scalpin'. I tell ya, the same bloke who did that, did the same to me. I know it for sure.'

Solo nodded back.

'Uh-huh, I'd be ready t' bet money on that myself.' He pulled up his neckerchief to cover his mouth and nose against the stench. 'I'll get him down and straightened-out ready.' Taking the old man's upper arm he led him from the scene. 'Why don't ya break out the shovel from the pack and make a start on a grave.'

Later, after Walt had self-consciously muttered jumbled but well-intentioned words over the grave, the two of them began a search of the place. Everything inside the crude cabin had been torn apart and wrecked.

'Don't get the wrong idea. Henry was always a neat little fella. A bit soft in the head, but gentle, like a mother. Wouldn't so much as step on a beetle,' the old prospector explained to Solo. 'It ain't right folks should treat him that way. All he ever did, when he wasn't pannin' gold, was pass his time makin' booze, playin' his fiddle and livin' in peace.'

Outside, at the rear of the cabin, Solo knelt and inspected the ground.

'Did Henry have any horses?' he asked.

Walt shook his head.

'No need for one. Walked everywhere he ever wanted t' go. Had a little burro though, to carry his jugs an' corn an' stuff for the booze.'

'Well that figures,' Solo announced. He pointed at the footprints in the soft earth where the sun had never reached. 'If ya look here you'll see tracks for three men, one of 'em's wearin' square-toed boots,' he pointed out. 'And over there's been horses and a burro or maybe a mule.'

'That'll he Henry's burro. They'll be usin' her to cart off some booze I expect.' Walt spat in disgust. 'I hope the first drop they drink chokes 'em, then burns their throats out. I hope . . .'

Solo paid little attention to his partner's ranting. Instead he followed the tracks of the long-gone horses. Then he pointed upstream.

'That's the way the murderin' coyotes took,' he growled as though to himself. Then he twisted round and as his anger boiled up, called out, 'Walter . . . let's you an' me get organized. Let's go after 'em.'

They spent the rest of that day melting lead, casting and trimming off extra minie balls, and cuttin out and greasing patches for Solo's flintlocks. By the time the moon shone overhead, preparations for the hunt had been made and both partners lay asleep in their bedrolls.

* * *

They hit the trail just before daylight. The sun was clawing its way up to set a halo on the furthest range of hill tops. In the valley the air was still chilled and a slowly moving blanket of white mist covered the trees and river. The dew lay wet and heavy on everything, man or God-made.

'I always was partial to this time of day.' Solomon Jackson said, taking in a deep breath.

'Me, too.' Red-eyed, Walter Krank yawned heavily and shuddered. 'I'm usually sleepin' like a rock.'

Apparently confident, the bush-whackers had made no attempt to cover their tracks. The trail was clear, and easy enough to follow from horse-back. Without warning the tracks turned sharply to the right, moved away from the river bank and plunged into the woods, leading towards a long range of hills further east.

'By my way o' thinkin', they're makin' a bee-line for Dead Bear Pass,' Walter voiced.

'A pass, eh? What's at the other end of it . . . d'ya know?'

'Not a lot . . . just miles an' miles of nothin' but mesquite and sagebush. Oh and . . . ' Walter stopped as soon as the words had left his lips. He gawped at Solo and thumped his fist into his palm. 'The stage line. That's it! That's what them varmints are plannin' on doin' next.'

'The stage?' Solo cut in, 'Yeah, now that seems a likely bet, don't it?'

'What day is it?'

Solo screwed up his eyes as he pondered.

'Thursday, I think.' Then he scraped at his chin and nodded. 'Yeah, it's Thursday all right. I shaved yesterday. Always scrape my whiskers off every Wednesday an' Saturday. And I know it wasn't Saturday. Why?'

'Thursday, that's definite then. It's the stage coach they're makin' a play for,' Walter persisted. 'It can't be anythin' else. If we aim t' prevent some more scalpin' and blood-lettin', we'll have to move fast. Usually it goes by the end of the pass round about noon.'

'Maybe the driver'll decide t' make a run for it?' Solo glanced at the old-timer. 'What ya think?'

Walt puckered his lips and spat out his well-chewed wad of twist tobacco before answering.

'Not likely. The team'll be plumb tuckered-out after haulin' that heavy Concord up that long slow rise.' He bit off a fresh chaw. 'Them horses'll be all frothed up an' blowin' like kettles, looking forward to change-over at the relay station. That's no more than two miles further on. And if my experience is anythin' to go by, them backshootin' outlaws'll not give 'em a chance to run.'

* * *

The sky clouded over, blocking out the blue, and the air had become more humid. The sun still climbed but was concealed behind the dark boiling clouds over half an hour before it reached its zenith.

Soaked with sweat, Solo and Walt rode cautiously through the dried-out mesquite clustered about the end of the pass. There was neither sight nor sound of the bushwhackers.

'Well, we trailed 'em here,' Solomon reasoned, mystified and scratching his head. 'There's no denying that. They've got t' be around somewhere.' Glad of the break from riding he slipped from the saddle. He walked ahead, eyes down, leading his mule while he read the sign. He stopped and pointed a little way to his right. 'I can't understand it. They ain't makin' any bones about it. They've gone straight for the stage road.'

Together they surveyed the area.

Away from the shelter of the hills, the grass had been sun-dried yellow and was in no way long enough to hide a crouching man, let alone a horse.

'We've guessed wrong,' Solo exclaimed. 'If they're gonna rob the stage they ain't gonna do it here.'

He had hardly finished speaking, when they looked at each other.

'The relay station!' The words were blurted out in unison.

'It's got t' be,' Walt agreed.

'Either that, or they ain't aimin' to rob the stage at all,' Solo added, staring to where the stage road converged before it disappeared over the distant rise. 'Maybe they've decided to mosey on t' some place else?'

The prospector had no chance to voice an opinion.

'This relay station,' Solo went on to ask, 'is there a way of gettin' close to it, without our heads bein' blown off?'

★ ★ ★

62

Solomon discovered a shallow gulch and, having followed it for a while, left Nelly there, munching on some scrub a quarter of a mile on the far side of the relay station. There was little time to spare. Already it was past noon and if he didn't hurry he would be too late to prevent a massacre.

The heat was oppressive and the distant horizon flickered with occasional flashes of lightning. The humidity increased his discomfort and he could feel a strange tingle in the air prickling at his skin.

Solo reasoned the outlaws would be concentrating their attention on the road, watching out for the dust cloud signalling the coming of the Concord. There was only sparse cover for the final hundred yards to the corral fence. The ground was as bare and flat as a kitchen table, forcing him to wriggle on his belly like a sidewinder, encumbered by his Kentucky long-rifle.

Distant thunder rumbled like cannon fire, and dark slanting grey streaks showed the first rain of the coming storm. By his estimation the downpour would reach him soon.

He detected no sign of life from either the relay station main building or the barn. Time passed. The sweat blackened the sun-faded buckskin on his back, while his crotch and armpits grew wetter from the perspiration leaking through from his own hide.

Dragging his shirt front open wider, he let the air blow on his skin, and glanced down the stage road towards the top of the rise. There was no sign of movement.

'Seems like the old-timer managed to stop the stage in time.' He grinned. 'Well, that ain't gonna please the fellas waitin' inside there.'

Another twenty uncomfortable minutes passed. He became aware of noises behind him and, checking over his shoulder, saw Walt accompanied by someone he assumed to be the guard from the stage. They were crawling towards him.

Walt's face beamed like a full moon as, panting with the effort, he brandished a borrowed cavalry Colt.

'We're ready when you are, partner,' he gasped. 'And we're all loaded up an' huntin' for bear . . . ain't we, Wilbur?' He nudged the fat guard who was busy mopping the trickles of sweat from his face and neck.

'Uh-huh, we sure are, mister,' he concurred, wheezing heavily as he dabbed continuously under his wobbling multiple chins. 'Gonna be a storm,' he mentioned as though no one else had noticed a further flash of lightning, quickly followed by a clap of thunder.

'You guys crazy?' snarled Solo. 'T' hell with the weather. Get down!'

Even as they flattened themselves to mother Earth, a stealthy figure emerged from the cabin and peeked around the corner, looking to where the stage should have appeared.

'That guy . . . he ain't one of the relay station fellas,' the fat guard wheezed. 'He don't belong at all.'

'Ye're right,' Walt agreed. Immediately he twisted his head to face Solomon. 'He's one o' them.'

'Ya sure?'

'I'll guarantee it.'

'In that case . . . he's dead.'

As the other two exchanged bemused glances, Solomon shuffled and spread his legs wide. Supporting himself on his elbows he settled into a comfortable firing position. Drawing back the hammer he levelled the long barrel, caressed the butt against his right cheek and peeped one-eyed through the backsight.

The rifle steadied, Solo's breathing stopped. His finger curled slowly round the trigger and squeezed. To the onlookers, it seemed to take an eternity for the hammer to flick forward, the powder to flash in the pan, and the gun to shoot.

Walt and the stagecoach guard, both tense with expectation, jumped with the sudden sound of the explosion. The blue-grey puff of smoke from the black powder had already begun to dissipate when they saw the inquisitive bushwhacker twist and slam back against the corner of the building.

Gradually the outlaw slid down, the heels of his riding boots ploughing furrows in the dust until he sat firmly on the ground and stayed there. When his hat fell off, his head lolled forward so that his chin rested on his chest, and remained still.

'Holy smoke! That was one hell of a shot, mister,' acknowledged the guard. 'No doubt about that.'

'One down,' Walt counted. 'That's nothin', ya should see what he can do with a difficult target.'

Solo merely rolled on to his side and kept low. More thunder and lightning heralded the coming storm. Carefully he carried through the complicated routine demanded for his muzzle-loader. Only when completely satisfied that all was as it should be, did he adopt the aiming position again, and wait.

A sudden movement captured their

attention. Another man came into full view in the doorway of the building.

'No!' The stage guard's cry was urgent. 'Don't you shoot him, mister. That's Charlie Cook, one of the company men.'

The trio watched as Charlie Cook raised his hands high and looking extremely reluctant, stepped out into the open. Close behind him, like a second skin, one of the bushwhackers held the muzzle of his pistol barrel to Charlie's temple.

'Whoever you are . . . ' yelled the sheltering gunman, 'any more shootin' from you, and this guy's brains'll be scattered like rice at a weddin'.'

'Keep your heads down. Stay still, and don't answer him,' Solo warned. 'It's likely they'll not know where we are.' Once again he prepared himself to fire if the opportunity presented itself.

Another hostage with his hands raised above his head appeared in the doorway, then stepped outside. The other remaining outlaw threatened him in the same manner as the first.

'That's Joe Cook . . . Charlie's pa,' the guard whispered. 'They both work for the company.'

'That's a surprise,' Solo grunted, laconically. 'What's the mother do?'

Slowly, walking the hostages backwards, the gunmen edged out of sight around the rear corner of the building.

Half a minute later, two shots were fired in rapid succession. Simultaneously, heavy drops of rain fell, sparse at first but quickly increasing in intensity, cutting down the visibility of the watchers. Then above the sound of the downpour, rapid hoof-beats informed him the outlaws were making good their escape.

Fully alert, Solo aimed the rifle to a point where he estimated the fleeing men would next appear. The raindrops, feeling as big as grapes, soaked through his clothing like bullets of ice, but be disregarded them.

By the time they had galloped clear from behind cover of the building, his targets were already at a considerable range. The leading horseman crouched along the neck of his cruelly spurred steed. Solo swung his thin-bladed foresight smoothly past him until he had allowed a sufficient lead. Grim-faced and still swinging, he squeezed the trigger.

4

The hammer of the Kentucky long-rifle sprang forward as another thunderclap echoed across the plain and rolled on into the far distance. The piece of flint, gripped in the leather-lined clamp, scraped down the steel frizzen, and, in spite of the wetness, still raised sparks. But the fine black powder in the pan, already soaked by a random raindrop, failed to ignite.

'Hell's bells!' Solo snarled and tensed in his frustration. 'Why now?'

'Try again,' urged Walter. 'It might go a second time.'

'It won't.'

'Go on. Try!'

Against his better judgement Solo recocked and aimed again. The hammer clicked, but still without the desired result. The rain increased, sheeting down in torrents, soaking them, causing hair and clothing to cling to their bodies and trickle its way into their boots. Even as they watched, the earth around them changed from dusty alkali into a sea of cloying mud.

Helpless, unable to prevent them, Solo watched the fleeing outlaws first become ghostly shadows in the downpour, then simply disappear behind the dark curtain of the storm.

'That damned old-fashioned flintlock!' Walter exploded. 'If ya weren't so pigheaded an' darned mean, and had had it converted t' percussion-cap, at least another one o' them backshooters would've met his Maker. And ya know it!'

Angered and dejected by his failure, Solomon Jackson made no pretence of defending either his gun or philosophy. Instead, with mud dripping from his clothes, he rose to his feet then, ignoring the deluge, splashed and squelched away from his two disappointed companions. Even before he had covered the distance to the relay station main building, he had come to a decision. Next time he found himself in town, he would make it his prime business to seek out a gunsmith.

With no more than a passing glance, he waded past the dead outlaw still sitting in a deepening pool of rainwater. Solo rounded the corner of the building and, although he had hoped to be proved wrong, was not.

There, close to a stout hitching rail, the bodies of both relay station employees lay crumpled and face-down in the mud.

'Bastards,' the stage guard groaned as he and Walter caught up with Solo and stared with revulsion at the cadavers. 'They didn't need t' do that.'

'Believe me, mister,' Walter attempted to console him. 'From what my partner an' me know of them bushwhackers . . . your friends . . . they got off lightly.' With those words spoken, he returned his attention to Solo. 'Well, partner, aren't ya goin' after them?'

Lifting his rain-soaked face to the sky

the mountain man wrinkled his nose.

'In this?' Solo looked down and nodded at his own footprints which were being rapidly merged into the rest of the sloppy mire. Curling his bottom lip he shook his head slowly. 'Waste o' time. This rainstorm, it'll wash their tracks clear away and put them at an advantage over me. And believe me, Walt, I ain't no fool hero. I don't aim to get my hide shot full o' holes, not when there ain't no real need to.'

'But,' protested the bemused prospector, 'what about Henry . . . and these other two fellas they've murdered?'

'Walter, I guess I've done me the eye-for-an-eye bit, an' evened the score for your pal, Henry,' Solo pointed out. Looking at the stage guard, he indicated the bodies in the mud. 'As for your friends, fella, you'd better see to it that either the stage-line or the sheriff take care of 'em.'

'And how about what them varmints did t' me, eh?' Walt yelled above the storm. 'Don't that count no more?'

'Yeah, it counts,' Solo replied crisply. 'Sure it does. But Walt, do me a favour, let me be the judge as t' how an' when I finish it.'

'But . . . ' Walter began, then said no more when Solo gave him the hard-eye and carried on talking to the guard.

'You'd better go tell your driver what's happened. Meanwhile, my partner an' me, we'll see to your two fellas and that outlaw.'

'Sure thing, you're the boss,' the company man agreed readily, glad not to have to take the initiative. Hauling his fat around, the cumbersome guard waddled off in to the storm as fast as he could go. Grinning all over his face, he was eager to break the big news to his colleagues and passengers waiting anxiously in the stagecoach down the road. He was lucky. All along the stage routes he would be famous. He had not fired a single shot. Yet he knew, that with a little verbal embroidery, such a story could, for years, be guaranteed to bring him free booze.

One by one the two partners carried the dead into the building and laid them in a neat row on the floor at the side of the short bar counter.

'Well, at least we've found some whisky.' Walter perked up and dodged under the bar flap. Grabbing a couple of glasses, he filled them from a part-used bottle. 'Here, wrap yer hide around this.'

Solo downed his, and twisting his features, gave Walt a wry look.

'Call that whisky? Hell, I wouldn't put that stuff in a lamp.'

After the third glass, the whisky did not taste so bad. By this time the stage had pulled up outside. In moments the passengers teemed in, gasped at the corpses and chattered excitedly like they had not spoken all year.

'Mind if I take your picture, gentlemen?' a smartly dressed dude asked. Even as he spoke, he was busy assembling a mahogany and brass camera on a heavy wooden

tripod. 'Harold C Porter's the name
. . . St Louis Picture and News Agency.'
with a deft shake, he opened a black
velvet cloth and draped it over the
rear of the camera. 'I make folks
famous.'

'We don't wanna be famous,' growled
the mountain man.

'Speak for yourself, I sure do,' Walt
butted in. 'I wanna be famous . . . an'
drunk.' He waved towards the camera.
'Hey, Mister Harold whatever-yer-
name-is. Is that one o' them newfangled
picture-takin machines?'

With a professional smile etched into
his features, Harold C Porter came
over, offering a thin, hairy-backed hand
to be shaken. His parted lips revealed
the soft yellow gleam of several gold
teeth, and his cologne was detected
from a yard away.

'Yes, sir, it certainly is. In fact
it's the very latest that photographic
science has devised.' He endured
Walt's pumping handshake for as
long as he could, then discreetly

withdrew his fingers from the horny-skinned grasp. 'The people out East want to know all about heroic men such as yourself and your big friend here.'

'Why?' For a moment the photographer was confused. He coughed, giving himself time to formulate an answer. 'Because they do . . . because they're Americans through and through. They're interested in you tough pioneering men . . . brave men who stop at nothing to open up the untamed Western wilderness of our great country.'

'Bullshit!' Solo leaned over the counter, grabbed the bottle and refilled his glass.

Noting his speech had made no impression on the buckskin-clad giant, he decided to change tack. 'Of course, I'm willing to pay handsomely for the privilege of taking your photographs.'

'I don't need money . . . I want me another whisky.'

'Whisky? Mister, I'll give you a case

of the stuff if you'll pose and give me a detail or two. I've a load in the boot of the stage.'

'Good stuff?' Walt perked up and joined in again.

'The best money can buy. It's all I drink.'

'Is that a fact?' Walt licked his lips as if he could already taste the booze. 'A case, ya say?'

'A dozen full bottles.'

'A case each?' Walter pushed.

The photographer winced, thought, then sighed.

'All right. A case each.' Then he bargained. 'If you'll give me your full story, tell me why you were here, and what happened . . . and how it feels to kill a man. And oh yes, it will have to be exclusive to the agency.'

★ ★ ★

'Got t' hand it to that picture-takin' fella,' admitted Solo one night as he sat by the cabin fire. 'This surely is

79

good sippin' whisky he gave us.'

Walter chuckled.

'In all my life that's the easiest an' best damned deal I ever done. My-oh-my, all that mighty fine booze for an hour's talkin' about nothin' at all.' Boisterously he slapped Solo on the back, and laughed. 'Ya know somethin'? I'm real tempted t' give up this gold-minin' idea, and make my livin' talkin' full-time to picture-takers from the east coast.'

'Talkin' of pictures,' began Solo in his soft Kentucky drawl. 'I wonder if that fella kept his word an' posted them copies care of the stage office, like he said? Ya know, I ain't never seen a picture o' me.'

'Well, we'll soon find out when we hit town next week,' remarked the old-timer. He uncorked the bottle again and poured two more drinks. 'We're gonna have us one hell of a shindig that day.' His eyes shone with speculation for the future. 'Just think on it. Next time we come back here, we'll have us a hired crew and we'll start a proper mine.'

★ ★ ★

Before weighing in and depositing their gold dust at the town's one and only bank-cum-assay office, Solo and Walter decided to book in at the biggest of the town's two hotels.

To their astonishment, the manager and his reception clerk greeted them as though they were royalty, bobbing their heads and gushing 'Yes, sir, no sir, and very good sir', to practically everything. Solo and Walter eyed each other, and wrinkled their brows, totally bemused. But it was the big mountain man who broached the subject first.

'Hey! What's up with the both of yers? Why all this dang fuss?'

'We know, sir.'

'Ya know?' Solo let his weighty saddle-bags slip on to the polished floor with a thud. He contorted his face and, deep in thought, scratched at the side of his jaw. 'Just exactly what d'ya know?'

Excited, the manager said no more, but proudly directed a quivering finger at the wood-panelled wall behind them. Having twisted round, they stared in total disbelief at a theatre poster advertising a play. Prominently displayed on it were photographs, and below these, their names. At the top, emblazoned in blood red, was the boldly printed title BANDIT KILLERS.

'Jesus!' Solo's face quickly lost its natural colour as he stood there gaping.

'I need a drink,' Walter whispered as in a dream he edged closer to the poster. After a time he asked, 'Do I look like that?'

'You surely do, Mister Krank, sir,' the clerk gushed. 'That's a real good likeness. I knew you both, the very minute you walked in through that there door.'

'You're too modest, gentlemen,' the manager butted in again, not wishing to be outdone by his minion. 'Surely, you must know? You're mighty famous right across the country. Why they tell me your names are spoken in every household from New York, St Louis, to Santa Fe . . . everywhere else, ever since the book of your daring exploits came out for sale.'

'Book . . . what book?' Again the partners looked aghast at each other and shrugged helplessly.

Without further bidding the manager ducked beneath the counter and emerged holding a copy of the volume concerned. It was embossed with the same title as the play and had been written by Harold C. Porter.

'The advance booking agent gave it to me at cost price, just for letting him put up that poster. He told me every spare room in town would be taken at premium prices, once that theatre tent goes up next week.'

'Talkin' about rooms,' Solo interrupted. 'How about ours, eh?'

'I've given you the best rooms in the hotel,' explained the manager, happily rubbing his hands and canting his head forward. 'If there is anything at all you require, gentlemen, just tug the bell-pull by your beds. Any time . . . day or night.'

'A hot bath each . . . with proper stinky soap that won't burn my hide off. And send up a barber,' Solo managed to order.

'And whisky,' insisted Walter. 'And send out to a store and buy us some longjohns. And remember . . . we ain't exactly skinflints. We'll be wantin' the best of everythin'.'

Later, in their bedroom, freshly shaved, trimmed and bathed, Solo and Walt relaxed in their soft new longjohns. Walt lay back on the bed, with his hands clasped behind his head. Contentedly he watched the smoke from his cigar as it twisted and curled lazily towards the ceiling.

'Well that easterner sure didn't tell no lies when he said he'd make us famous,' Walter declared. Suddenly he heaved a sigh. Rolling over on to one elbow he grinned at Solo across the gap between the two beds. 'Feels kinda good, bein' knowed . . . don't it?'

'Yep, dandy. Like every day's a Sunday.' Abruptly Solo sat up, swinging his feet to the floor. 'Hey, we've got t' get that gold dust over the bank.' Already he was climbing into his pants. 'Come on, we'll both have to check an' sign for the account.'

'Aw heck, leave it 'til t'morrow.' The old-timer scowled.

'No!' Solo dragged his buckskin shirt on over his head. 'We ain't gonna take the risk of some gunman bustin' in durin' the night an' holdin' us up. No sir, I don't aim to risk losin' everythin' now.'

'Oh, suit yourself. Ya know, sometimes you're a real pain in the butt.' Walter shuffled off the bed. 'But after we've done with the assay an' made the deposit, what say we mosey along t' the saloon and have us a good time,' he suggested. 'Agreed?'

'Uh-huh, I ain't gonna kick against

that idea, Walt. Who knows, maybe we'll have us an hour or two with some gals.'

* * *

'Say, mister, don't I know you from somewhere?' a bare-shouldered saloon girl asked, appearing from nowhere and slipping easily on to Solo's knee. Seductively she wrapped her arm round his neck.

'Maybe,' he answered, making no objection to her antics.

'On the run from the law? Your face on a Wanted poster or somethin' . . . eh?'

'Like I said, maybe.'

'Hey, I know you an' him.' She nodded across the table at Walter. 'You're both on that poster they've been sticking up all around town. I just knew I'd seen ya's.'

'Well, now you've just seen us again.'

The young brunette continued speaking, while she fingered his freshly shaved face and sniffed his hair. 'You've had a proper bath. You smell good.' She twined her fingers in his locks. 'You rich?' she wheedled. 'Or just different from the other fellas round this hell-hole?'

From the other side of table, shrieks of a woman's laughter were heard. Walter's own drunken laugh cackled along with hers as the heavyweight blonde pressed his face to her more-than-ample bosom. She giggled, her podgy fingers tickling and teasing him all the more.

'Ya want t' die in there, old man?' an angry male voice shouted above the bar-room noise. 'Ya will if ya don't take yer friggin' nose out from Maggie's tits.'

At once the normal hum of conversation in the saloon died. People froze, not sure which way to move. Only the out-of-tune piano tinkled on as before. But even the half-drunk player became aware of the silence after a while. Gradually he let his fingers slow down. Then the tune stopped altogether.

'Old man,' the grating voice persisted. 'Get yer friggin' nose out o' there.'

The big blonde had ceased her girlish shrieks at the first warning. Now scared and embarrassed, she heaved herself up and pushed away from the befuddled Walter.

'He's only a harmless old man. He wasn't doin' anythin' wrong, Joe.'

'Shut yer mouth, bitch, and stand clear.' Joe thumbed the holster loop clear of the hammer and eased his Peacemaker in the leather.

In response, there was an immediate scraping of chair legs on the bare-planked floor. Those in close proximity to the antagonists wasted no time in evacuating the danger area.

'What's the problem?' Walter blinked around to see where the blonde had gone.

'No problem,' Solo answered quietly. 'Just you sit a while.'

Joe shifted his gaze to Solo, and

twisted his thin, consumptive features into a sneer.

'Who emptied a bucket into your trough, mister?'

'Now you go steady there, young fella-me-lad,' Solo cautioned, as gently but firmly he lifted the slim brunette from his knee and shoved her clear from any danger. 'My partner wasn't harmin' anyone. No need t' bust a gut or start a rumpus over nothin' at all.'

'Who asked you? Shut yer lip, mountain man. If ya wanna live long enough to get back t' yer stinkin' squaws, just keep that big nose o' yours out of my business,' Joe threatened.

A further noisy flurry, and more chairs and tables were pushed or bumped aside as worried onlookers behind Solo rushed out of the way.

With no hint of fear, but with a determined set to his jaw, the mountain man pushed back his chair and stood taller than anyone else in the saloon. Angled across his belly, with the softly-shining black barrel stuck through his belt, his Kentucky pistol was clearly visible.

The stranger, no doubt used to having things his way, seemed intent on throwing his weight about. He pointed at the old-fashioned muzzle-loader and laughed outright.

'Hey, you guys,' he called to his cronies standing by the bar. 'Seen this fella's artillery?' With scorn he stared Solo full in the face. 'What the friggin' hell d'ya think you're gonna do with that . . . start a foot-race or somethin'?'

One or two in the bunch leaning on the bar had witnessed the drama develop with the same inevitability as night following day. One laughed nervously but stopped at once when Solo resumed speaking.

'Mind how ya use yer dirty loud mouth in front of the ladies . . . boy.' The quiet, easy drawl of the Kentuckian would have warned anyone with more than a lick of sense, that he had stopped fooling around. 'Ladies don't enjoy that sort of talk . . . it ain't nice.'

'Ladies?' Taken aback, Joe stared wide-eyed, laughed again, then snarled his defiance. 'I'll say any damn thing I like in front of these shagged-out whores.' Totally convinced of his own superiority as a gunslinger, and certain his own modern revolver was more than a match for any old flintlock. Joe played to the gallery and smirked.

Smoothly, his gun hand snaked into the ready position, his elbow bent and held out a little. Slender leather-gloved fingers quivered only slightly as they flexed into hooks, and hovered a mere inch clear of the Peacemaker's butt. The tied-down holster informed everyone that this was a game he had played before and always won.

'It's your privilege t' eat crow shit, or call, squaw-man.' He leered, and hunched his narrow shoulders. 'So . . . any time ya feel like dyin' . . . ' Joe leaned forward, grim-faced and tensed like a trap spring. 'Just say . . . go!'

5

'Go!' Solo's snapped-out response, loud and immediate, served to confuse his challenger. Startled, Joe grabbed for his gun.

In a blur of motion, the mountain man bent his knees and twisted slightly to one side. As his right hand gripped the easy curving butt of the pistol, he pressed down. The barrel twisted in the leather belt and pointed up squarely at the chest of his adversary. Already his left hand fanned the hammer back while his trigger finger squeezed.

Belching smoke, the long barrel thundered and bucked as if alive. Joe staggered back, his Colt Peacemaker hardly clear of its holster. His eyes rolled wildly. He attempted to speak but gagged. Instead of words, blood gurgling from his lips mixed with that already staining the front of his fancy white shirt. As though frosting over, his eyes dimmed and, as he collapsed, his face bounced on the floor. The gun clenched in his fist fired a solitary bullet harmlessly into a half-full spittoon by the bar.

The leaking spittoon stopped spinning. After a timeless moment of silence, during which only the ticking of the painted German clock behind the bar could be heard, Solo resumed his seat and calmly set about reloading his pistol.

At the other side of the table, Walter sat, his whisky-reddened eyes unblinking under puckered brows, staring at Solo in wonderment.

'Somethin' botherin' ya Walt?'

Walt jerked himself back to life.

'Flintlock or not, ya sure are fast, son.'

Footsteps hammered on the wooden steps outside. The swing doors burst open and the sheriff dashed in with two deputies close on his heels. Gripped in both hands he carried a double-barrelled twelve gauge, with both its hammers drawn back. He swept the weapon round to threaten everyone there. Walking forward until he reached the brand new corpse, he gave it a cursory glance.

'Well, if he had any troubles, he ain't got 'em now. Who did it?' the lawman demanded curtly. When no reply came he rubber-necked around the room. 'Who killed this man?' His attention settled on Solo, who, unconcerned, was busy ramming a minie ball into the Kentucky pistol. 'You shot this man?'

'Well, kissin' him wouldn't have saved my hide,' Solo drawled with an obvious sigh.

'Put that gun down, I'm takin' you in, fella.'

'Oh! What for?'

'Murder . . . that's what for.'

'Murder, my arse!' Indignant, Walter staggered to his feet and stood swaying while his partner carried on tending to his task. 'A blind mule with its brains stove in could tell it ain't no murder. It's a plain an' simple case o' self-defense.' Expectantly he appealed to the others in the saloon. 'Well, boys, y' all saw it. Is that the gospel truth, or ain't it?'

The barflies exchanged awkward glances, but no one wanted to be the first to speak up. With superior smirk creasing his face, the sheriff nodded as if to say he thought as much, then savagely jerked his shot-gun to indicate Solo should rise.

'Joe asked for it, Sheriff,' the busty blonde stated. 'He was hell-bent on havin' a fight. He called the big guy out . . . but he lost fair an' square.' She indicated Solo with a sideways cant of her head. 'That there stranger, he was too good an' fast for him by a long mile.'

'That's the way it was. The gal's tellin' ya nothin' which ain't the truth,' the bartender joined in.

'Sheriff, ya should've been here an' seen it,' a ranch hand blurted out. 'That mountain man's shootin' hand . . . fastest darned thing I ever did see. Hell, he moves it quicker than a rattlesnake's pecker.'

This broke the ice. All of a sudden it seemed everyone else wanted to get in on the act, and embroider it more. Annoyed yet helpless under this noisy onslaught of witnesses in favour of Solo, the lawman ungraciously lowered his scatter-gun and uncocked it.

'Jacko . . . an' you too, Abel.' The sheriff beckoned to a pair of well-built youths leaning against the end of the bar. 'You boys take this here body along to the funeral parlour. Tell the undertaker, I say the county'll pick up the bill.' As the youths hesitated, and glanced at their partly drunk beers on the bar-top, he yelled, 'Move it . . . now!'

'Hold on, Sheriff.' Solo's countermanding call once again brought the saloon to an expectant silence. The sheriff peered over his shoulder at him with suspicion.

'Yeah?'

'The dead guy's hand-gun.'

'What about it?'

'Who does it belong to now?'

'Well, he ain't got no kin, I know that for sure. So I guess the county'll take it, along with his horse, an' the rest of his belongin's. Everythin'll be sold off at auction, t' pay for the funeral and his cemetery plot. Why? What's it to you?'

'I've got a proposal . . . if yer willin' to go along with it.' Solo did not wait for a reply but went on to explain. 'I'll pay for a decent funeral, providin' I can have his gun an' rig in exchange.' He paused while the lawman toyed with the ends of his moustache and pondered on the question. 'Well, Sheriff, what ya say?'

'Just his gun an' rig . . . not his horse or nothin'?'

'That's what I said. Just give the word, and the county should show a profit on the deal.'

The sheriff stooped, unbuckled Joe's

gun belt, and picked up the Colt Peacemaker. Bundling them together, he handed them to Solo.

'You've got a deal. Drop round at the office and I'll write ya an official bill o' sale.'

Having demonstrated his authority, the lawman curtly jerked his head at each of his sidekicks, twisted abruptly on his heel and marched with heavy steps from the saloon. His deputies, like whipped dogs, followed at his heels, leaving Solo and Walter to enjoy more free drinks than was good for them.

* * *

Word of the shooting travelled faster than a prairie fire. Coupled with this, their pictures shown on the many theatre bills spread around the town, enhanced Solo and Walt's reputations. Speculation increased when, dressed in new clothes more suitable for mine owners, they advertised in the local newspaper, to recruit workers to take back with them.

Within days, men who had joked about them when Solo had first entered town dragging Walter on the travois, now afforded them the utmost respect. Hats were raised and women still smiled and nodded, but more hopefully now that the newcomers were spending and had the smell of wealth about them.

They had bought and paid for their second flat-bottomed cart along with a suitable team of mules. Having completed the deal, Solo asked the seller for his advice.

'Who's the best carpenter around?'

The merchant answered without hesitation.

'Dick Hickory. There ain't no doubt about it.'

'Where do we find him?'

'The funeral parlour. Dick makes all the coffins.'

Within half an hour, despite the pleadings and threats of the undertaker, Dick was on their payroll and had already gone home to pack his tools and things.

'Strange, ain't it?' Walter grinned, after he had raised his new hat in response to a similar salute from a townie. 'The difference a pocketful of dollars makes in the way folks treat ya? It don't seem no time at all since they used t' look down their noses at me.' He twisted round to Solo. 'Guess that never happened t' you . . . on account you're so much longer in the legs.'

★ ★ ★

Two wagons piled high with mill-sawn lumber, vittles, and various tools and implements for the mine, trundled out of town. Along with them went Solo, Walt and their eight hired men.

The loaded wagons had made it impractical to travel the trail Solo and Walt had used on horseback. Instead, they were forced to make a much longer detour, using the stage road until they reached the turn-off at Dead Bear Pass.

'Wait, ya know somethin', it's kind of excitin'. I like the feelin' of gettin' rich,' Solo remarked. 'Funny . . . never reasoned it that way before.'

'Son, I've dreamed about it ever since I was nothin' but a snotty-nosed kid,' Walter answered. 'I've worked for it all my life. Now I want t' sit on my arse for a while, and let other folks run about doin' my biddin' for a change.' He gazed thoughtfully into the distance and after a while whispered, 'Yeah, an' it's startin' t' happen now. Solo, we're on our way.'

The trek had been tiring. Having arrived at the claim, one day's rest was allowed before work was to be started in earnest. The two partner did not need any real discussion on how things should operate. Walter knew the technicalities of the mining business best, so he selected the most experienced men to work the mine.

Armed with picks and shovels, they

began to open up the doorway of a drift in the cliff face. This opening would, in time, branch off into several tunnels, each sloping down to different levels into the bowels of the earth.

Because of his particular skill with wood, Dick Hickory was given authority by means of a man assigned to work under him. Their first task was to build extra living quarters and a cookhouse, all to be ready before the freezing grip of winter closed in.

Using the percussion-cap-adapted long-rifle, Solo shot fresh game daily. he also removed the fish from the Indian pattern trap he had constructed with osiers, and positioned where the river narrowed. Any surplus food, he dried or smoked for leaner times during the winter.

Acting as the general manager, working flat-out in all he did, he kept an eagle eye on the others felling timber in the woods.

At spare moments he practised in private with the Colt Peacemaker, getting the feel of the balance, and quickly gaining confidence and ability with that weapon.

Summer, and then fall, slipped by. It was important that they kept up a regular supply of felled timber for both the building and the many extra roof-supports required each day in the mine.

One morning as the cookhouse triangle sounded its clamorous signal for breakfast, Solo awoke to find the first frosts had arrived.

'It won't be long before the white stuff comes down,' the mountain man remarked. 'Back there in the mountains the whole place will've been snowed-in an' frozen solid for more'n a month.'

'It can snow as much as it wants,' Walter gasped as he sat on the edge of his bunk, struggling into his pants. 'We've done real good since we got back here. The winter won't stop us none.' He grinned. 'By the time spring comes around again, we'll be in to the real pay-dirt and buyin' and riggin' us a crushin' mill, to grade the rock down.'

'And then what'll we do?'

'Do?' He chuckled as he often did. 'Son, we'll go t' town again, raise hell and hire more men t' dig us a bigger mine. The way things are pannin' out, we're gonna be richer than I first thought.'

It was a few days later. So far although the frosts were quite severe, only a light dusting of snow had fallen. Solo had been away from the mine hunting for meat, and was making his way back. He was on foot, leading Nelly. Slung across her back was a bunch of turkeys and a mule deer stag, all shot by the Kentucky long-rifle.

Suddenly something caught his attention. He stopped in his tracks at the top of a bluff, overlooking the mine and living area.

Impatient to get back to her stall and nose-bag, Nelly moved forward to snuffle and push her muzzle at the back of his neck as Solo knelt to inspect the frozen ground.

'Now, Nelly, you behave, can't ya

see I'm busy?' He pushed her away and picked up three well-smoked cigar butts with teeth marks embedded clearly in them. Peering closer he whispered to himself. 'Mmm, one broken tooth, eh?' He felt the burnt ends, smelled at each one and squeezed them gently between finger and thumb.

On closer inspection of the immediate area, in different places away from the edge, he discovered several yellow urine stains, splashed up on some frosted rocks. Further away, among a thick stand of birch, hoof prints and horse droppings told him that someone's shod mount had been tied and concealed there for some considerable time.

'Well, Nelly, I don't know who, but it looks like somebody's mighty interested in what we've all been doin' down below.' Clicking his tongue a couple of times he tossed the cigar butts aside and waded on through the snow with the mule following.

'Saw ya messin' round up on the ridge,' Walter mentioned as they sat down to eat a while later.

'Uh-huh, I think we can expect company.'

The old-timer as though half expecting the news, barely reacted.

'Trouble?'

'Seems that way. Some guy's spent quite a while under cover, spyin' on us from up there.'

'Indian, maybe?'

Solo shook his head with some vigour.

'If it was I wouldn't be so worried. We ain't got much of what an Indian would want.' He shook his head again. 'No, Walt, it was a white man. One who likes t'smoke cigars and has a chunk of a front tooth broken off.'

'Mexican cigars?' Walter looked worried.

'Yeah, that's right. Not too fat, strong smellin' like burnin' boots, an' nearly black.' Solomon noted his partner's serious expression. 'Think ya know the guy?'

'It's one of them same bushwhackers

again.' Walter's grip increased on his knife handle. In a surge of anger he stabbed the blade deep and savagely into the table top. 'I'll say I know. I'll never forget 'im. He's that squinty-eyed galoot I told ya about. The one who laughs like a jack-ass, and farts like a horse.'

★ ★ ★

Solomon Jackson organized a rolling rota system. All winter long, every man stood guard for two hours at a time. Constantly on the alert, he himself made searches at irregular intervals, covering all around the mine area. A number of times he came across various signs informing him that several different men had been spying on them, but that was all. In his own mind he was certain a bigger gang than just the original bushwhackers was involved.

'Why they holdin' off, that's what I'd like t' know?'

'Walt, it sticks out like the nose on yer face. This is a workin' gold mine, ain't it? Folks know we'll have to ship our gold out some time, so what else are they gonna do, eh? They'll wait 'til we do just that . . . then they'll hit us and hope t' clean us out.'

'Well we can't just sit on our butts and wait for 'em t' rob us blind. At least, I ain't.' The old-timer forgot all about his half-eaten meal, pushed back his chair and left the table, his features flushed with anger. 'And if you aim to let them backshooters take what we've worked for, well, son, I'll be real disappointed in ya.'

Solo carried on chewing at his food with slow deliberate movements of his jaw, and taking time to think before replying to the old man's charge. Finally he raised his head.

'You finished mouthin' off?'

His partner pressed his tobacco-stained lips together, shuffled his feet and spat in to the fire. He looked guilty, but adamant.

'You've heard what I said,' Walt retorted at last. 'You ain't deaf.'

'Well maybe you are, so just rein in yer horse an' listen t' me for a change.' Wiping the last of his sourdough biscuit round his plate, he mopped up the gravy and stuffed it into his mouth. Only when he had chewed it well and swallowed it, did he attempt to speak again. 'You know the guys we have workin' for us. Tell me, how many of the fellas here have guns and can use 'em? Or would put their lives on the line and use 'em, just to save the gold?'

Pondering on the question for some time, Walt heaved one of his expressive sighs and shrugged.

'How am I expected t' know that? Maybe four or five, at a pinch would have guns . . . but I wouldn't know for sure if any would be loyal enough t' stand up an' fight.'

Pouring two more refills of fresh coffee, Solo pushed one steaming mug across the table towards Walt.

'Don't ya think it's time we laid it on the line for the crew, and find out how they feel?'

'Fair enough. I'm game to go along with that. Them that want to, well . . .' He shrugged and displayed with his hands. 'We'll give 'em any wages due and they can shove off right away.'

'And them that don't?' Solo queried.

'We'll reward 'em. Give 'em a bonus on account o' the extra work they'll have t' do. Yeah, and let's give 'em a raise in their wages.'

Solo stood in front of the men assembled in the cookhouse after breakfast next morning. For five minutes he had been explaining the situation.

'We don't expect the gang will try to make a move before the thaw sets in. Their boss . . . he won't be a fool. He'll know we won't be making any shipment before then, so I'm pretty certain we can take it easy until the spring.' He spread his hands. 'Like I explained before, if ya want t' leave . . . no hard feelin's. No one's gonna stand in yer way.'

Three of them decided to pack it in. They were married men, each with families, and didn't feel it was right to take risks in anybody's fight but their own. The others, made of tougher stuff, were content to leave their fate in the lap of the gods, and welcomed with cheers the proposed extra pay they were promised.

★ ★ ★

Shortly after the meeting had broken up, a bored man, with a pronounced squint, puffed at a Mexican cigar and shivered as he crouched behind a rock. Barely interested, he observed the mine workers leave the cookhouse, split up, then disperse to their various jobs. However, not long afterwards he bucked up and took more notice when three riders rode out together, away from the mine. They took the easy route for that time of year, along the frozen river.

On closer inspection through his military-style eye glasses, he saw to his consternation that their mounts were well loaded, each with saddle-bags stuffed tight. Also, each man was dressed warmly as if for a long journey. And maybe, more to the point, all three were headed downstream, taking the direction which would lead them towards the nearest town.

It was, the watcher decided, just possible that the trio could be carrying a shipment of gold through by the short route instead of using the pass.

Squint could feel his excitement rising. Quickly he considered the newly altered situation, weighing the odds of his skill with a Winchester against three miners who, as likely as not, had no idea of gunfighting. Not only that, but the element of surprise was on his side.

The main spur to his consideration was the distinct possibility of raw gold in the offing. The outlaw was sick and tired of being a nobody in the gang, receiving only a miserable share of any booty. But with plenty of gold behind him, he could break free. He smiled, dreaming of a rosy future.

'With a whole heap o' gold, I'd be the guy who does the jawin'. I'd be boss-man of an outfit.' In spite of the crisp cold, the palms of his hands began to sweat at the thrill of potential danger. His mind was made up.

'What've I got t' lose?' he muttered. 'Nothin'! Yeah . . . it's a good bet.'

Crafty as a fox, and very conscious of the need to remain concealed from his quarry, he kept his head below the skyline. Carefully retreating, he was glad of an excuse to abandon his uncomfortable watch position.

In a crouching run, ignoring the thorny branches scratching at his cheeks, he pushed and crashed through the trees and leafless bushes, cursing the dislodged snow, from branches above, which fell upon him. In a narrow clearing bereft of trees because of the rock-covered ground, his horse stood waiting, head down and miserable with nothing but the chill wind for company.

Without a thought for the welfare of the animal, Squint leapt into the saddle. Jerking the reins so hard that the animal reared in pain, he used the ends to lash the horse's shoulders while he kicked his spurs into its flanks until blood coloured the star-shaped rowels.

Galloping, weaving through the snow, skilfully avoiding the natural obstacles, he risked his life and limb to ride in a direction which he knew would cut across the long bowing course of the river below.

This would save him both time and distance, and allow him to draw ahead. Already his mind buzzed with plans for the preparation of his ambush of the three miners.

6

Where the frozen river narrowed and bent to pass between the granite cliffs, a rifle barked its message. The leading rider of the departing trio crumpled sideways. This surprise action as he gripped on to the reins, unbalanced his mount and twisted the horse's head so that man and animal fell over heavily together.

Down on his side, with his leg still across the saddle, and his heavy work-boot securely held in a stirrup, the miner lifted his head as if to see where he was. Without a word being uttered, he let his head drop back again. Before the rumbling echoes of the first rifle shot had faded into oblivion, the miner's wife was already a widow.

Spooked by the noise, the second miner's mount reared and plunged. Its rider, barely comprehending what was happening, fought frantically to control it and stay in the saddle. When finally its back legs slipped and splayed on the ice, the gelding went down on its haunches, unseating its inexpert rider, sending his sprawling on to his back.

Another bullet struck home, bowling over the third prancing horse as it jinked to avoid the animal struggling in front of it. Mortally wounded, it crashed down on to the first man's head and shoulders, crushing his beneath the weight of its hindquarter, and spilling the third miner on to the blood-splashed ice and snow.

'Harry . . . Elmer's dead!' screamed the second rider, as if he could not believe such a thing. 'And, some bastard's shot my horse.' Terrified out of his mind, he struggled manfully, hauling on the reins to get the dead man's animal back on to its feet.

From somewhere above, keeping safely out of pistol range about seventy yards ahead, the unseen rifleman fired again. The second rider knew he was wasting his time. The animal, having struggled to its knees, rolled back over on to its side again. Screaming, it shuddered and kicked its life away.

'Forget 'em,' Harry yelled. 'Come on, ya damned fool. Let's you an' me get t' hell out of here.' On foot, he grabbed the only horse left alive. Ducking low, using the massive body as a shield between him and the rifleman, he ran alongside it, upstream, back towards the mine.

'Harry! Wait . . . wait for me,' gasped the other man pounding along, trying desperately to grab the horse's tail to help him keep up.

His arm was still outstretched when the bullet split the top of his spine as though chopped by an axe. Head-first he dived and slithered. Ploughing a furrow in the snow which carpeted the ice, his momentum carried him along after the horse. Then he slowed and stopped in its tracks . . . dead.

'Yah, yah, yah!' Harry urged the

horse to greater efforts, never once looking back. He could hardly breathe from the exertion of taking giant strides while hanging on grimly to the girth. Ahead lay a dog-leg bend in the river. If only he could reach its cover? 'Yup, horse,' he panted. 'Yup!'

Vaguely, Harry wondered why his left arm flopped at his side as he ran with the horse. He became conscious of a strange burning pain and something like warm gravy flowing down the inside of his coat sleeve.

The horse collapsed so suddenly that, if Harry had not dragged his hand free of the girth, he would have fallen with it. Another bullet flattened as it gouged flesh from the dying mount's rib-cage. Another slug zinged noisily past his own head.

Ducking and weaving to spoil the gunman's aim, he made for the corner of the bend. Twelve yards to go. A further fusillade of hot lead ricocheted from the granite cliff face. Although cursing his luck, this simple fortuitous act had saved his hide from the next bullet.

In one last half-crazed scramble, he wormed between scattered rocks and around the bend, out of the killer marksman's field of vision. With his chest heaving and his breath rasping in his throat, Harry closed his eyes and thanked the Lord for allowing him this temporary sanctuary.

★ ★ ★

'Ya hear that, boss?' Dick Hickory asked Solo as they loaded a flat handcart with cut timbers ready to be taken into the mine.

'Gunshots!' Solo answered. 'Seems them fellas who just left have run into a whole mess o' trouble.' Already he was setting off at a run to collect Nelly from the stable. 'Warn Walter an' the others, Dick,' he yelled over his shoulder. 'Tell 'em t' get in position like we planned. Get the guns out. Keep 'em on their toes.'

Following the departed miners' tracks was a simple enough matter, but Solo did not dash along blindly. There was no sense in having a hole blasted through his own head by an unseen assassin. It was better to live as a coward than be a dead hero, any damn day.

Solo had heard no further gunshots since having ridden from the mine. In his estimation that bare fact pointed to only one thing. Those first bullets must have been all that were needed to do the intended job.

He pressed on, only slowing again when he spotted the exhausted figure staggering towards him. Raising his head, the man saw him and, appearing to gain strength, suddenly moved faster, waving one arm, signalling him to stop.

'Mister Jackson . . . sir?' The call was one of relief, yet at the same time the figure looked back fearfully over his shoulder. In not much more than a whisper-loud gasp, he pleaded,

'Don't shoot . . . it's me, Harry.'

Having dismounted, Solo glanced past Harry, to check downstream, but saw no one following.

'What happened, where are the other fellas?'

'Back there.' Harry nodded wearily behind him. 'Dead . . . bushwhacked.' In a state close to collapse, he swayed and would have fallen if Solo had not caught him. 'Never stood a chance.'

'OK, Harry, save yer breath, there ain't nothin' ya can do about it now.' Sitting the miner on a boulder by the river bank, Solo warned him, 'Now you keep yer eyes open, ya hear? Look over my shoulder, in case any of them backshooters are comin' after ya, while I take a gander at this arm o' yours.'

Slitting the bloodstained sleeve with his hunting knife, Solo quickly attended to the bullet-shattered arm. Scraping snow from the north side of a rock, he found some moss growing and utilized this to stop the bleeding. Holding it on the wound, he bandaged it firmly with

Harry's own necktie.

'That better?' Already, he had devised his plan of action.

'Yeah boss. Thanks.'

'Reckon ya can make it back to the mine on foot?'

With his confidence restored and, as if to prove he could, Harry got to his feet. Although his face was still pallid, he produced a grin.

'Uh-huh. See?' He executed a few comic steps. 'Easy!'

'Good. That's a comfort. I wanna use Nelly to catch up with the guys who shot ya.'

★ ★ ★

'You stay here out o' the way,' he growled softly, leaving the mule concealed on the river bank. Sidling along through the undergrowth, he made for the spot Harry had described. Having seen where the cliff jutted out into the river, his Colt, loaded in all chambers, was already gripped firmly in his fist, and its hammer thumbed back to full cock.

Big as he was, his former years of hunting in the mountains had taught him how to move as silently as a cat walking on velvet. Using every scrap of cover, he eased himself closer to the bend. Breathing lightly, he held himself alert and ready to respond to the slightest movement or sound.

A lone horse lay on its side on the ice, its great head pointing in his direction. The tongue lolled out over the partly dislodged nickel bit, and there was no movement of the barrel-chest. Neither was there breath steaming from its black gaping nostrils. Any one of these observations along with the bloodstained snow, would have told him that the animal was definitely dead.

At a glance he saw that the saddle-bags, bed-roll and a gunny sack had been opened and were now empty. Faded pink long-johns and an assortment of personal possessions, a frying pan and coffee can were scattered carelessly around on the ice. But whoever had done the killing and looting was already gone.

Crouching by the dead horse, Solo was now able to view a similar scene of carnage and robbery further downstream. Swiftly his eyes followed the trail of blood spots which led past the nearest horse and on to the mound of rocks where the miner had hidden for a while.

'Guess this's about where Harry caught that bullet,' he reasoned aloud. Quickly dispelling the thought from his mind, he concentrated upon the clear footprints pressed into the snow, recognizing them at once. Square-toed, they belonged to the spy with the weak bladder, the guy who had a liking for smoking Mexican cigars.

A further check revealed where Squint had left the river to climb the bank and return to his horse.

'Right . . .' The mountain man nodded. Reholstering his revolver, he

124

scanned the track leading diagonally up to the top of the cliff. 'This time no misfire's gonna save ya, fella. Yer dead!'

Ignoring the bodies, he half ran in long loping strides, like an Indian, to collect his mule from where he had left it. She was waiting, ears pricked as he emerged from the bushes. In one springing motion he straddled the decorated saddle and reined her towards the frozen river.

'Move it, Nelly. We've got work t' do.'

Surefooted, the white mule carried the mountain man along the ice, then later, just as easily, climbed the track like a mountain goat. In no time at all they had reached the plateau and were cantering along in the wake of the murderer.

★ ★ ★

Squint gritted his teeth. There had been no gold to fulfil his personal dreams. The fistful of dollars and a silver pocket watch he had taken from the bodies would buy a few nights of steady drinking, and maybe a time or so with a bar-room whore, but that was about all. It had hardly been worth the effort, but then, life was cheap.

The biggest disappointment was in having to delay his plans, and return to the gang's hideout. His only consolation was the knowledge that this time he had been able to grab all the profit for himself. What could go wrong? There was nothing to worry about.

Concluding that dead men don't hunt the living, and not wanting to arrive back too soon, he rode along at an easy walk.

Making no attempt to conceal his tracks, Squint gazed with satisfaction at the sky to windward and smiled sardonically. Any fool could see the darkening clouds gathering. Soon there would be more snow. The dead would be covered, and all tracks obliterated without any effort on his behalf. And later on in the year, when the thaw finally arrived, all evidence of the murders would be washed away downstream with the floodwater, and that would be that.

★ ★ ★

Standing out sharply against the slate grey of the skyline, Solo spotted the silhouette of the killer walking his mount along a ridge which led towards Dead Bear Pass. A surge of elation rose within the mountain man, and for once he drove his heels into Nelly's flanks, urging her forward to overtake his quarry.

Taking advantage of every ripple in the ground, Solo gained on Squint. By the time the first snow flurries arrived he had worked his way past him and, finding a suitable spot, dismounted. Calmly he waited, listening, standing to face the direction the bushwhacker would come from.

Having estimated Squint's position by sound alone, Solo hefted the Colt Peacemaker, and held its barrel rock-steady. Then he stepped out to confront the lone outlaw who had ridden around the corner of a bluff, into close pistol range.

'Get 'em up high,' Solo called loud and clear.

Utterly surprised by the challenge, Squint let his half-smoked cigar fall from his mouth to sizzle out in the snow. He pulled up, and for a second or so, looked as though he would reach for his gun. But instead he dropped the rein and slowly raised his hands to shoulder level.

'High, I said.'

Squint, by virtue of his previous spying missions at the mine, had already recognized the mountain man. Slowly he pushed his gloved hands way above his hat.

'What ya playin' at, fella?' he bluffed. 'Ya aimin' t' rob me?' Laughing he went on, 'Holy shit, that ain't fair. You'd be robbin' yer own. I'm an outlaw myself.'

'Keep yer hands up and slide down from that saddle. An' see ya move real slow.'

The self-confessed outlaw shrugged and did as he was bid.

'What ya aimin' t' do? I ain't got anythin' you'd want, so keep that finger good an' loose, I ain't worth killin'.'

'Believe me . . . to me, ya are.'

The grin melted from Squint's face.

'Eh?' he gasped, turning paler with each passing moment. 'What ya mean by that?'

'I'm gonna kill ya.'

'Me . . . why? What've I done to you, fella?' A worried whine had replaced Squint's bombastic voice. His mind raced, preparing to plead and promise anything in exchange for a chance to live.

Solo shook his head.

'You've done nothin' t' me.'

'Well then,' Squint butted in, relieved,

'what's all this crazy talk about killin' me, then?'

'Ya scalped a good friend o' mine, and killed some others. That's why you're gonna die.'

Squint's lower jaw sagged. He dribbled, and began to back away, his master eye fixed upon Solo's Colt, his other closing, while his arm lowered inch by inch.

'Ya can't shoot me down . . . not in cold blood . . . that would be murder in any court o' law.'

Solo laughed but did not relax his gaze. Making a show of it, he uncocked the hammer and returned his pistol to its holster.

'Glad t' know the law impresses ya so much. It'll be that much easier to dole out my kind of justice.'

That was when Squint chose to make his play. His right hand whipped down, grabbed the carved bone handle of his gun and jerked it clear of leather.

Solo's private practice sessions paid off. His weapon fired a fraction ahead in time. The heavy bull-nosed .45 slug grooved along the wrist before smashing the elbow of the outlaw's gun arm.

'Aaah!' Squint screamed in agony and dropped his unfired pistol into the snow at his feet.

'Jesus, gi' me a chance mister,' he squealed, tenderly caressing his bleeding and damaged limb with his other hand. 'I'd do the same for you.'

'Sure ya would,' Solo sneered, shooting a hole through Squint's other arm. 'You should've been a preacher . . . you give everybody a chance, don't ya?' The Colt barked again and the bushwhacker fell to the ground blubbering and writhing due to a shattered kneecap. His other knee soon suffered the same fate.

'Please, mister . . . ' Squint begged. 'No more, no more.'

'Yeah, just one more,' Solo said coldly, raising the pistol in line with the other's head. 'This one's a slice of justice for my partner, the old-timer you scalped and pegged out on the plain for buzzard meat.'

From five yards away, impassively lining up the sights, he ignored Squint's fear-filled eyes. Rock-steady, Solo gently squeezed the trigger.

Bang! The hand-gun kicked back and the muzzle jerked up a fraction. As though by some magic trick, a small round hole appeared in Squint's grimy-skinned brow, and the head slammed back into the snow. His eyes had rolled upward so that only the whites were showing, and a thin trickle of blood oozed from the newly made hole.

Soft silent flakes of snow began to fall as, devoid of emotion, the mountain man turned from the scene, holstered his gun and strolled back to the mule.

He had done what he had set out to do. The miners who had died that day had been avenged, and their killer sent galloping along the never-ending highway to hell.

7

Spring arrived abruptly that year. One night everyone at the mine had gone tired and cold to their beds, and with frost an inch thick on the windows. But when they awoke next morning, the sun shone like there had never been a winter. And everywhere around, melt water dripped noisily and at an increasing rate from countless icicles.

Within days the melting snow retreated and long-forgotten greenery broke through, expanding its dominion by the minute. Several bears were noticed, thin and scruffy after their hibernation, and daily, skeins of noisy geese flew overhead on their return to the lakes to breed.

The sheet-ice broke up in the river and, swollen by melt water, the roaring torrent carried it speeding and foaming down towards the plains.

Solo, conscious that the winter was over, knew the danger of attack from the bushwhackers would increase. He took to making more rounds of inspection in the hope that he ould come upon one of the gang's spies. If he could do that, capture him and make him talk, he might have a stronger hand to play. Many times already he had cursed himself for shooting Squint without interrogating him. But that chance had gone.

'See anyone up there t'day?' Walt asked one evening after work was done.

'Not exactly . . . somebody's been around here, watchin' same as before, but they ain't takin' many chances. I don't think they'll wait much longer.'

'What ya reckon we should do, son?' Walt asked as he tucked into a plate of rabbit stew. 'The boys who've stayed on, they've worked like coolies and earned that bonus we promised. Now they're actin' like prize roosters, fair itchin' t' get their hands on some wages and hit town. Yes siree, they're droolin' at the lips for some hard drinkin' an' a chance to do some foolin' around with lively womenfolk of like minds.' He paused with his spoon in front of his mouth and gave Solo a wicked wink. 'An' knowin' you an' me, I guess that goes double for us.'

Rocking back in his chair, Solo placed his hands behind his head.

'The way I see it, whatever we do is bound t' be risky with those outlaws still hanging around . . . watchin' every move.'

'Everythin's a risk. Hell, I've got me some gold and I want t' spend some, same as the boys.'

'Wait . . . just havin' gold's not enough. You've got t' be alive to spend it.'

'They didn't kill me last time,' Walt countered. 'An' believe me, they tried hard enough.'

'Maybe they've learned a thing or two since then,' Solo growled. 'Remember, they managed real well with your old pal Henry.' Leaning forward earnestly he raised a cautionary finger. 'And then, they only had three members in the gang, but now, not countin' the ones I put under the sod, from different signs I've seen, the gang's growed t' half a dozen at least.'

The old-timer scowled and noisily scraped his plate clean with his spoon. He finished, licked the spoon, then poked it at Solo.

'Ain't ya forgettin' somethin'?'

'Like what?'

'There happens t' be seven of us.'

'And only five guns between the lot of us . . . ' the mountain man reminded. 'An' three of them belong t' me.' His chair scraped back across the floor-boards as he stood angrily. 'That don't quite make us an army, does it, eh . . . well, does it?'

Walter scowled again and turning his head, puckered his lips and spat loudly into the fire. Having done what he had to, he heaved a sigh.

'You're a good shot, I know that,' Walt wheedled. 'I've seen how good.

And ya said yourself how ya'd won all them turkey-shootin' competitions. A big clever fella like you, if ya set yer mind to it, why ya could lick the livin' daylights out of that gang o' no-goods, all on yer ownsome.'

Embarrassed by his partner's simple faith in his abilities, Solo grinned.

'Walt, ye're a caution. Next, you'll be tellin' me ya still believe in the tooth-fairy.'

The old-timer broke into a smile.

'Funny ya should say that. I surely do . . . an' Santa Claus.'

★ ★ ★

To get surprise on their side, Solo arranged for everyone to steal away from the mine one morning while it was still dark, well before sun-up.

'Quiet,' he warned. 'If we can move out without the fella up there seein', it'll give us that much more headway.'

With nothing to transport to town, and the two flat carts running light, the teams made good progress. By daylight they had already penetrated well into Dead Bear Pass and each man's spirits and hopes rose along with the sun.

Solo had chosen to ride alone along the cliff-top on the eastern side of the pass. That way he had the sunlight behind him, and could also keep an eye on the convoy below. In the unlikely case of the gang attacking them on horseback, he'd be ready. But most important of all was his ability to see a great distance ahead, his keen eyes seeking signs of ambushers taking up firing positions along the rugged tops.

Any likely trouble, Solo assumed, would be on his side of the pass, but the ambushers would not be expecting him.

By the time the noonday sun was beating down into the pass, the mountain man himself was beginning to believe he had dreamed up the danger. He drew Nelly to a halt and dismounted to give her a drink from his hat before quenching his own thirst.

Replacing the stopper in the canteen, he sensed rather than saw movement in the distance.

Shading his eyes he peered through the shimmering air, concentrating on the area he had been attracted to. For a time he saw nothing. Then it appeared again. It made jerking movements from behind some wind-carved boulders set back about sixty yards from the edge of the pass.

'Well, just look at that, Nelly,' Solo muttered as though the mule completely understood his every word. 'Judgin' by all that head tossin' an' shakin' over there, it seems like somebody's horse is being pestered by hungry flies.'

A few meandering bends still concealed the approaching wagons from the apparent ambush. Riding close to the edge, he waved his hat down at the wagons. When Walt gave an answering wave, Solo moved his own extended arm a number of times in a pre-arranged signal, passing on the

139

direction and distance of the outlaws' position.

Satisfied those in the carts knew what was expected of them, he remounted the white mule and rode away at right angles to the pass. Only when sure he could not be seen by the gang, did he turn on to a parallel course. That way he could curve round and attack the ambushers from behind.

'Let's get goin', Nelly, you've been gettin' too fat, it's time ya earned your hay.'

★ ★ ★

Unhurried, he cat-crawled the final two hundred yards from where he had hidden the mule. Closing in to range, Solo gritted his teeth, listening as his prey joked and laughed.

'Ya can have yer fun, boys,' he whispered grimly resolving to do the job as planned. 'But none of you'll be laughin' party-style when I'm through.'

Checking from position to position,

he counted seven men, each crouched behind safe cover, where the edge of the pass curved into a rough semicircle giving them a good view of the bottom. Clutched in their hands or lying on the rocks beside them, their pistols and rifles were ready and waiting for the bloodbath to commence.

Some distance behind them, in a secluded spot thirty-five yards to Solo's left, and unseen by anyone travelling through the pass below, the outlaws had left their mounts.

From the semi-shade offered by a barren pile of sun-heated boulders, he recognized the same tormented horse which had drawn his attention earlier. The animal was still fretfully tossing its head, stretching its neck and shaking its untidy mane.

Nearby, its uncomfortable companions, long overdue for a shearing, sweated and looked tatty in their rough winter coats. Occasionally they bared their teeth or kicked out at those alongside them. Others stood with mournful sagging heads, and lashed their flanks constantly with swishing tails, hoping to clear the avaricious blood-sucking flies.

Scanning the tethered animals, Solo sensed something not quite right. Frowning, he counted. Eight! At once, accepting the possibility that he had made a mistake, he re-counted the bushwhackers, but came to the same conclusion as before. Seven!

'Well, seven fellas can't ride eight horses.' Solo scraped at his whiskers with his finger-nails. 'If the eighth guy ain't with the others . . . he's gotta be somewhere close enough t' be on foot.'

The rattle of carts and clicking of iron-shod hoofs on the rock floor of the pass drew his attention back to the current situation. At the same time, talking and jesting stopped apparently without any order being given as the gang's guns were taken up again and trial-sighted. In about two more minutes the flat carts would be almost within point-blank range.

Solo flicked up the back-sight until it clicked home, then slid the long barrel of his modified Kentucky rifle through a convenient gap between the boulders. Automatically he observed a tuft of sun-dried grass growing about halfway between himself and his selected target. The grass bent only slightly in the light breeze, but mentally he still made allowance for it as he took aim.

Solo's first selected target was to be the bushwhacker placed furthest away from him. He was the one most likely to make the opening shot when Walt and the miners came into view below.

The target suddenly came to life and leaned out a little way over the rock to aim his Spencer carbine down into the pass. But before he was able to fire a single round, his hat flew off and spun out of sight as the top of his head was splattered and lifted by a minie ball. Unfired, the Spencer carbine slithered and clattered down the cliff face on to the rocky floor of the pass.

Without bothering to recharge the muzzle-loader, Solo placed it beside him while he cleared leather with his newfangled Colt and selected the next man in the gang to die.

Startled by the shot from behind, each outlaw twisted round, craning his neck to locate the threat. When Solo's Colt spoke its message of doom, the second outlaw threw up his arms and stood for a moment, his hand-gun pointing at the sky. Then the weapon wavered and dropped from his fist as he changed into a corpse. Collapsing, he spread-eagled and draped himself neatly over a rock like a recently laundered set of longjohns laid out to dry.

By this time Solo was aware of muffled shots being fired from those with guns on the wagons now speeding at full gallop through that section of the pass.

Unnerved by the unexpected change in their fortunes, the bushwhackers were obviously undecided on what action to adopt. Some kept heads down and

144

protected their hides, others shot wildly at the unseen enemy, while a couple, conscious of their own vulnerability, loosed off a few half-hearted rounds in vain at the rapidly disappearing miners.

Despite a natural urge to hurry, Solo tenaciously took his time, aimed and fired twice. Each round drilled a hole through bushwhackers shooting down into the pass. But these last two shots, though successful, had betrayed his position.

'There he is,' someone yelled. 'The bastard's hidin' in them rocks.'

A storm of gunfire came Solo's way. All around him bullets gouged pieces of rock before screaming away overhead. Others ricocheted and bounced dangerously several times off boulders, forcing him to duck low and hug the ground.

At the first slight lull he snapped off a couple of shots back, then attempted a third but the hammer only clicked dully as it fell on an empty chamber.

'Damn! Should've counted.' Rolling

on to his back he was about to reload when a boot crunched, rattling some small rocks behind him. Out of the corner of his eye he saw the silhouette of the eighth man against the sunbright sky. The man's gun-hand was already raising to take a bead.

Solo froze. A wave of raw, intense fear gripped him as he realized there was no way he could retaliate in time. Life hung suspended as he lay watching the grinning man slowly line him up in his sights. Hypnotized by the outlaw's finger as it tightened on the trigger, he gathered all his strength.

Pure animal instinct caused him to attempt a twisting sideways lunge out of the line of fire. But something went wrong. He knew that as soon as a million needle-sharp flashes of light blinded him. Instantly he suffered an overwhelming tide of pain, and became vaguely aware of an explosive blast.

The needle-sharp lights evolved into a swirling glow of fire. He was falling, tumbling over and over, down into a

146

bottomless pit. He could hear laughter. It was all round him, loud and jeering. Then the fire-glow faded. The light went out and everything was silent leaving only the pain.

★ ★ ★

'He croaked?' asked the gang leader.

'Not yet he ain't,' smirked the one who had shot Solo. 'But he sure as hell's gonna be.' Thumbing back the hammer of his hand-gun he aimed at Solo's stomach.

'No! Hold it, Jake.' The leader stepped down from the rock beside the comatose mountain man. 'I've got me a better idea.'

'Aw, hecky-me, boss. He ain't gonna make it. He's good as dead already,' Jake objected, whining like a disappointed child. 'Look what he done t' the other fellas.'

The boss simply stared at the would-be executioner, over the inert form of the injured man.

'Ya disagreein' wi' me, boy?'

Jake looked awkward and uncomfortable as he realized the other gang members were hanging on his reply. He flushed, shrugged and with ill grace replaced his gun in its holster. His head gave a couple of shakes.

'Naw . . . not worth arguin' about, is he, boss?' Head down, avoiding the others' eyes, he stepped back. 'I mean, no skin off my nose.'

The boss already had his back turned, and was busy casting his gaze around those other men who remained alive after Solo's shooting. He focused on a half-breed youth.

'Billy-boy.' He pointed an imperious finger at the breed who, like the others, grinned at Jake's discomfort. The breed's grin vanished like snow on a hot branding iron, and he dedicated his full attention.

'Boss?' was all he said.

'Ya can do me some trackin'. Try an' find this smart-arse's horse, put 'im on it and bring 'im back to the hide-out.'

'Sure, boss.' Without another word, the breed left to search for Solo's tracks.

'An' Billy-boy . . . be careful. I want him brought back alive. I'll have yer balls if I don't. Savvy?'

'Savvy.' The grin returned and he looked hopeful. 'You torture, yeah?'

The boss laughed.

'Let me do it, boss. Same way my tribe does it.' The breed's dark eyes sparkled. 'I keep him alive . . . long long time.'

'Maybe, ya blood-thirsty heathen. But you'll have t' wait a while, until I've made me a real handsome profit out of his mangey carcase.'

8

A torrent of pain accompanied Solo back to the land of the living. Eyes tightly shut, he endured a piercing hot agony such as he had never known. Even the slightest move of his head threatened to rip the top off his skull.

He became aware of the stench of stale vomit. When the urge to spew could no longer be resisted he wretched, but brought nothing up. That was when he realized that the drying vomit plastered over his chest was his own.

A different kind of pain infiltrated his legs and arms as severe cramp spread through. Attempting to ease them, he discovered it was impossible to move. Each limb had been securely roped to the wooden frame of the lat bed on which he lay.

Suddenly a much harsher pain caused him to call out and strain violently against the ropes. This new agony clung on, and there was the distinctive acrid stench of burning flesh and hair. Still writhing, he forced his eyes open and stared into the evil grinning features of Billy-boy.

The breed still leaned over him, a smoking cigar butt held in his dirt-encrusted brown hand, only an inch or so above the mountain man's hairy chest. The pink tip of his tongue protruded as, with evident delight, he slowly lowered the burning end of the cigar again.

In spite of the mind-daunting pain in his head, Solo could not tear his gaze away. A crop of hairs curling out from his chest suddenly sizzled and shrivelled, shrinking from the heat. He could hear them. Wisps of blue-grey smoke drifted up, and he smelled the burning again. Sweat beaded on his face and ran in streams down his cheeks as the breed continued to reduce the distance between the red-hot butt end and the skin at the base of the sprouting hairs.

All the while the breed smiled as he moved the cigar slightly to one side, introducing it to a fresh unscorched area.

Solo bore the torture in silence for as long as he was able, but at last was obliged to gasp out and yell.

'Bastard!'

'That's right . . . my pa was a white man,' the half-breed snarled. 'A mountain man, same as you.' Again the cigar descended among the shrivelled hairs and the prisoner bit his lips against the pain.

'What in the name o' holy hell!' The voice sounded from a few feet away, angrily loud and coming closer. 'Ya damned no-account stupid mongrel, I told ya not to harm him.'

The dark eyes of the breed flashed briefly, demonstrating a mixture of hate and defiance towards the owner of the voice. But this show of bravado quickly altered to a display of fear.

A hard-balled fist seemed to appear

from nowhere and struck the torturer full in the mouth, knocking him off the edge of the bed to sprawl headlong on the floor.

'Now get up an' get yer heathen arse out of here. An' don't try that game again, 'til I tell ya. Right?' As the downed man was slow to respond, the gang boss balled his fist again, belligerently stepped a couple of paces closer to the breed and glared down at him. 'I said . . . right?'

Billy-boy, keeping his eyes on the white man, felt at a newly loosened front tooth with his tongue as he shuffled his backside along the floor away from trouble. Dragging his brown hand roughly across his mouth, he wiped at the blood, smearing it across his cheek. Reluctantly he rose to his feet.

'Right, boss. I ain't likely t' forget that.' The cold way he said it seemed to make the gang boss uncomfortable. So much so that the latter modified his tone.

'Well, just you see ya don't.' He pointed to the door. 'Out!'

The pains in Solo's head took charge of his body again. His brow wrinkled into deep furrows and he closed his eyes. Then once more he spiralled down out of control, plunging into the maelstrom of screaming darkness.

* * *

'What's eatin' Billy-boy, boss?' Jake asked as he came into the room and joined the man staring at the unconscious prisoner. 'Ya give 'im a flea in his ear, or somethin'?'

'No . . . got himself a good punch in the mouth . . . lucky I didn't kill 'im, the damned fool.' Resting his chin thoughtfully in his cupped hand, he frowned, staring down at the figure on the bed, the half-breed already forgotten. With curled fingers, he worried at his bottom lip. Heaving a sigh he shook his head. 'Don't like the shape o' this fella.'

'Same goes double for me,' Jake answered. Then a grin erupted and spread wide. 'He wouldn't look so good dressed in some o' them frilly white drawers, would he? Myself . . . I always had me a strong leanin' towards them busty straw-haired dance-hall gals.'

The gang boss sneered disdainfully and fixed him a sad-eyed withering stare.

'Ya know, Jake . . . ye're sick,' he said quietly. 'This ain't the time to be makin' smart-mouth jokes.' He strolled round the bed. 'No time at all.' Twisting round to face Jake, he indicated Solo. 'If this guy cashes in his chips, we can all kiss goodbye to a fortune.'

Jake half-closed an eye and, deep in thought, picked at his fight-twisted nose with his finger and thumb, carefully considering his boss's statement.

'A fortune, boss . . . ?' Perplexed, he twisted his pock-marked face. 'How? I just don't get it. We missed out on that gold shipment didn't we, eh?'

★ ★ ★

Once the wagons carrying Walter Krank and the miners had been driven safely out at the other end of Dead Bear Pass, he called a halt. Every man watched the opening to the pass, waiting anxiously for Solo to turn up. Long hours dragged and the sun travelled all the way across the sky. But still the mountain man had not shown.

'Maybe he's not comin',' suggested Harry, still nursing his bullet-deformed arm in a sling.

'Well, nobody's bullet-proof,' another man mentioned. 'He could've been shot dead.'

'That's right,' Harry chirped up again. 'It's real easy gettin' shot . . . I should know. Maybe his luck's run out. Maybe he'll never get here.'

'Shut yer damned fool mouths,' Walter barked, both worried and angry. 'We're stayin' right where we are. Solo told us he'd meet us here, an' I believe 'im.' Standing on the leading cart he

156

pulled down the brim of his hat until it shaded his eyes. Determination showing in the set of his jaw, he blinked against the sunset behind the cliffs on either side of the pass. 'Ain't never knowed Solo t' tell an untruth yet . . . not even in fun.'

As darkness fell and the temperature began to drop, Walter grudgingly admitted to himself it did not look good for his partner. If he and his men had been well armed, he would have felt justified in backtracking to search for Solo. But with only a couple of hand-guns between them, he had no right to ask them to run such a risk.

'OK, boys, climb aboard. We'll keep to the stage road and make for the town.'

'Huh! Then what?' muttered Harry to the man sitting next to him. Walter heard.

'We'll call on the law, that's what! Maybe this time we can persuade that no-account sheriff to get off his political arse an' round up a posse.' Peering through the gathering darkness at the silent miners, he added, 'If he don't, I sure as hell will . . . and I'll be expectin' volunteers.'

A hiss of whispered asides began from those sitting on the rear of the wagon, but quickly stopped when Walter twisted around on the driving seat to face them. With anger in his words he spoke clearly and with venom.

'And I'll want 'em all carryin' guns, an' them that don't . . . don't have jobs.'

* * *

The yellow glow of the oil lamp faded, having been replaced by the brighter light of dawn. For the umpteenth time Solo regained consciousness. But on this occasion the pain in his head was not so severe.

'Wanna drink, fella?' The words sounded harsh, yet his thirst was far too great for him to refuse the offer.

'Yeah,' he managed to croak.

A surprisingly gentle hand held up his head, and a chipped enamelled tin mug was pressed tenderly to his lips. The water had been drawn from a spring and he recognized the taste of sulphur and its offensive stench of rotten eggs. But it was refreshingly cool so he drank gratefully.

'Shove-off, squaw,' the harsh voice commanded. Solo's head rested back on the pillow, and raising his eyes he was just in time to see a slender Indian girl move out of his field of vision.

The speaker must have noticed the surprise in Solo's eyes. He chuckled.

'Well, you're sure on the mend, fella, takin' notice of White Fawn like that.' He licked along the gummed edge of a cigarette he had rolled, stuck it and delicately smoothed it with fat sausage fingers. 'Can't say I blame ya. She's got the sort of shape that could bring a corpse t' life. It was her who fixed yer head.'

'Why am I here?'

'Because that's what Cradock wants.'

'Cradock . . . he your boss?'

'What d' you think?' The other sneered striking a match to light his smoke. 'Most of us just wanted t' blow ya away. But him, he says we all got t' treat ya good.' Inhaling deeply on the cigarette, he held his gaze on Solo. 'Says ya worth money.' Blowing out his smoke in a powerful stream, he took another drag and again inhaled deeply. 'That right, is it?'

'What's it to you, Hagger?'

Hagger jumped back and away from the bedside as though he had been stung.

'Didn't mean nothin', boss. Makin' small talk, that's all.'

'Out!' The gang boss jerked his thumb towards the door.

'But boss, I . . . ' Hagger started to argue but thought better of it, stopped and left the room without risking another word.

Cradock grinned at Solo.

'See the sort of scum I've got to deal with? Can't get any good help at all these days . . . not since the war.'

Solo did not return the crooked smile. Instead he went right in headlong.

'Why?'

The outlaw lifted one foot and placed it on the side of the bed, then rested his hand on his knee.

'Ya mean, why I've been kind an' generous enough t' save your hide?' He waited, expecting an answer of sorts. As none came he continued. 'Like Hagger said, my guess is that your partner'd be ready to part with a whole heap of dollars just to get ya off the hook.'

'Huh! Ya crazy? What makes ya think I'm a partner?' Solo growled.

The gang leader sighed in mock sadness as he shook his head.

'Mister, I give ya fair warnin', don't make the mistake of believin' I was born short on brains.' Suddenly he pointed his forefinger like a pistol and aimed it right a Solo. 'You and the old man, ya both go about spoutin' an' givin' the orders at that mine. I know, 'cos I've seen ya. Besides that, the both of ya share the same cabin, separate from the men.' Cradock smiled smugly at his own reasoning. 'Now, unless you're a nancy-boy, I'd say that you an' the old man, you're partners for sure. And fella, even with that long curly hair, ya don't look like no nancy-boy t' me.'

Solo scowled and looked as if to make a move.

'Go, on, huff an' puff as much as you like, it'll not do a mite o' good. That rope'll hold an ox.'

'Are ya crazy? I need the privy,' Solo explained. 'I'm warnin' ya, unless ya want this shack to turn into one, you'd better let me pay a visit.'

Hagger and another bandit accompanied him as, hog-tied, he shuffled across to the broken-down two-hole privy set well away from the cabin. Inside, fending off the buzzing flies, he utilized some of the time by taking peeks through the many knot-holes in the weather-warped and split boards, trying to recognize his location. But it was all to no avail.

As far as Solo could make out, the hide-out was set well back in a canyon boxed off by an enormous rockfall. This barrier looked man-made, as though someone had blasted the sides of the canyon with powder or dynamite. As far as he could see, forty feet high or more, steeply-faced sandstone cliffs protected the hide-out from prying eyes.

Pegged against the sun-baked face of the cliff opposite the cabin and stables, Solo made out a roughly constructed wooden ladder lashed together with rope. Patrolling back and forth along the ridge above this a sentry, armed with a carbine, kept look-out.

On the southernmost side, in the permanent shade close to the cliff beside the cabin, a spring bubbled up from the rock floor to form a long narrow pool. As soon as he saw this he knew where his cooling morning drink had come from.

Someone's boot kicked, and a clenched fist hammered hard on the privy door. Immediately a miniature avalanche of dust and crumbling wormwood fell from inside the roof.

'Cut it out!' Solo yelled angrily, choking. Blinking his eyes in the dust cloud and spitting out the grit, he sneezed forcefully several times, and ran his fingers through his hair. Once again blinding lights flashed behind his eyes and the heavy pains returned. Feeling carefully, he tried to remove filthy debris from the wound dressing White Fawn had tied.

The men outside were laughing. Then the kicking and banging on the door was repeated just as loud as before, and one of the guards shouted, 'Hey, mountain man. Come on, hurry yourself up. What the hell are ya doin' in there . . . playin' around, thinkin' on our little squaw?'

The privy was spinning round as the pain increased inside Solo's skull. The door appeared to be coming towards him. He collided with it. As it slammed open he fell outside, and sprawled unconscious at the feet of the surprised outlaws.

* * *

White Fawn was the first person Solo laid eyes on when he came to. Sad-eyed, she bathed his face with a cold, wet rag, reminding him of another Indian girl way back in his youth. He smiled at her and she returned it but only briefly.

'That'll do, woman,' Cradock growled. 'Get out of here an' get on with yer work, before ya get him all worked up like a randy jack-rabbit.'

The young squaw took up her bowl and silently slipped away from the bedside. Solo tried to watch her go but could not, having been securely tied down again. He sighed audibly.

'Ya have t' rope me like a steer at brandin' time?'

'You bet,' the gang boss answered, coming into view. 'I'm a cautious man. That's why I'm in control here an' you ain't.' Then he laughed quite pleasantly. 'Fella, I don't mind admittin' you had us all mighty worried for a time after you passed out at the privy. We all thought you'd booked in for Boot Hill.'

'I'm real touched,' Solo drawled sarcastically. 'Maybe I should call ya Momma.'

'Yeah,' Cradock went on, ignoring the jibe. 'Again the boys all saw that gold vanishin' before their eyes. I tell ya . . . we was all real sad.'

Suddenly he reached behind his back with one hand. When he brought it back into view it held a knife.

It was a big knife. A heavy hunting knife which only the day before had hung at Solo's waist, behind his gun holster. The outlaw boss spat on the palm of his left hand. Then, slowly he began to strop the great steel blade on the spittle-wet skin.

'That's one thing I'll say about mountain men, you all keep a blade in prime workin' condition. Yes sir, a fella could shave with a weapon such as this.'

'I often do,' Solo confirmed, wondering what all the preamble was leading up to.

'Did,' corrected the other. 'I'm the only one who's gonna do any cuttin' with it from now on.' For a moment he stopped his steady stropping action and expertly felt the edge with the ball of his right thumb. 'Mmm, not bad, but it'll get better.'

He spat into his hand again and his careful stropping recommenced slowly and methodically, without feeling, like a machine.

Something was going to happen soon. Solo sensed it. It would not be pleasant or to his advantage, that was certain. He became aware of people entering the room. Their foosteps shuffled and scraped on the floorboards and blue smoke from a cigar drifted across the ceiling.

A couple of the arrivals came closer. Solo recognized Jake and Billy-boy. Jake wore a grim frown and licked at his lips a lot. But the breed, he just kept on bright-eyed and smiling like it was party-time.

'OK . . . hold him still, boys,' the boss commanded, having tested the keenness of the blade once more. Wiping the spittle from his hand and the knife on the seat of his pants, he advanced towards the bed.

There was little point in Solo attempting to struggle. Apart from the ropes which restricted him, Jake leaned his weight on his chest and held his shoulders down with his hands. On the other side of the bed, the half-breed gripped Solo's jaw with both hands and held his head rigid.

The pains resumed along with the flashes of light as he watched the knife blade draw closer to his face. Behind the blade he could dimly see the teeth-gritting leer of the outlaw boss.

'Now, mountain man . . . ' Cradock breathed heavily. 'We'll see what ye're made of.'

9

The outlaw boss did not stab or slash quickly with the hunting knife. Instead, he lingered over the job, seeming to savour each movement, taking his time, moving the blade as an artistic chef would slice a fine ham.

Solo having expected to die, was surprised as the razor-honed edge slowly parted his flesh. Never before having been purposefully cut, the intense but bearable sensation shocked him.

Then it was all over. The watchers round the bed cheered, and he was still alive. In front of him the blade hung vertically, dripping his blood from its point.

For what seemed an age the knifeman held it there, leaning over Solo and inspecting his handiwork with satisfaction before straightening up. Standing tall and still facing him, Cradock signalled to his helpers.

'Holy smoke!' Someone out of Solo's sight, broke the silence as the breed and Jake released their holds and stood grinning down at him.

A stream of warmth flowed down the side of Solo's neck, trickled under his head, then soaked through his hair and into the pillow.

'That's ten bucks ya owe me, Billy-boy,' Jake chortled. 'Told ya didn't I . . . he's not the sort. Said he'd not scream out.'

'Stop shootin' yer mouth off, Jake.' The man with the knife wiped the blood from it on to the blanket at the foot of the bed. Only when satisfied that the weapon was perfectly clean, did he return it to its sheath. Then he called out again. 'Billy-boy.'

'Yeah, boss?'

'Go an' fetch me a bottle of corn-whisky from my room . . . an' think on, I know how much's in it.'

Still numbed, Solo could not fully

comprehend what had happened. Or why? The flashing lights were more subdued. He breathed easier now and the flare-up of pain from the bullet-wound reduced again.

When the half-breed arrived back with the bottle of whisky, Cradock withdrew the cork with his teeth and swaggered over to stand by the head of the bed once more.

'This'll do ya a whole heap o' good, Mister Mountain Man,' he promised. The outlaw boss, without ceremony, tipped the bottle. There was a gurgling noise. The golden liquid swilled freely over the side of Solo's head.

'Jesus! My ear . . . it's burnin' like all hell's been let loose.' Solo's involuntary outburst caused a wave of laughter. The alcohol had brought the smarting back with a vengeance. Its fierce sting forced tears to his eyes.

'What was that ya said?' Jake grinned broadly. 'What ear's that yer talkin' about?' Mockingly he cupped a hand to the side of his head as though he was going deaf. Suddenly he held out the bloodied ear between finger and thumb for Solo to see. Then the awful truth dawned.

'You miserable bastards!' His pain temporarily forgotten, he contemplated his deliberate disfigurement. Through gritted teeth he snarled, 'I'll get even . . . with all of yers. Every single one of you mangey coyotes. Just see if I don't.'

Cradock hawked loudly then spat on the floor.

'Mister Mountain Man,' he muttered quietly, 'if I was you, I'd be mighty sure to keep my mouth shut tight.' Wagging an admonishing finger, he winked and spoke across the bed to Jake. 'You think I'm wrong?'

'Hell, no, boss. Ya knows ya ain't.' He turned to Solo. 'Fella, we don't usually do things this way. I tell ya straight, ya don't know how lucky y'are.'

'See . . . what did I just tell ya? Now that's real good advice I've been a-givin' ya for free. So ya better take note. Otherwise . . . well, let's see now. You've another ear. A big handsome nose, some lips . . . oh yeah, and a whole bunch of fine curly hair.' Then his grin widened. 'And of course, there's always yer little old pecker sittin' there, warmin' its clutch o' eggs.'

* * *

Walter Krank's temper blazed as he confronted the same bone-idle lawman he had seen the last time he had been in the town.

'Call yourself a lawman?'

'Nope. I call myself the town sheriff.' His face was already turning purple as he shoved his chair back. Banging his fist on his desk as he stood to confront the old-timer, spittle bubbled white on his mean, twisted lips. 'Town Sheriff!' He bawled the words loud enough to be heard halfway up Main Street. 'I told you an' that big hill-billy last time you stopped by this way. Bein' town sheriff's what I get paid for. Ask the mayor, he'll tell ya. Anythin' outside the town boundaries . . . just ain't my business.'

'Well you've got authority. Ya can call in the army or somethin', can't ya?' Walter suggested in his despair. 'Surely ya can do that much?'

The sheriff stood transfixed. His jaw dropped open as his eyebrows arched towards his hairline. At first he wore a look of utter amazement. Then he laughed and, although they did not know why, his toadying deputies leaning against the far wall laughed with him.

'The . . . army?' he gasped at last. 'Ya want I should call out the army . . . for one lousy man?'

'And why in tarnation shouldn't ya? Ya say yer a sheriff, you've got the authority. That's what the army's there for, to protect the people of these here United States,' Walter reasoned. 'They ain't busy. They ain't away fightin' a war, are they?'

'You're downright loco, ya know that?' The sheriff grabbed his hat and buckled on his gunbelt. He jerked his head for his deputies to follow. 'Come on, boys. Time t' do the rounds.'

'But what about my partner?' Walter persisted. 'If you won't do nothin' t' help, who will?'

The sheriff shrugged.

'Go to the telegraph office. Send for the marshal. He's the guy who deals with out-of-town shenanigans.' As he pushed by Walter to leave the office, he smirked. 'The marshal gets paid better, too.'

'An' how long will he take t' get here?' the old-timer asked. 'The marshal?'

'Him? About a week . . . if he puts himself out t' be real quick,' the lawman answered. A few swaggering steps further on, he yelled over his shoulder, 'Course, it may be three or more if he's busy. And if he's real busy . . . well, mister.' He bit off a plug of tobacco and chewed at it a couple of times before tucking it inside his cheek. 'He'll just forget all about ya and you won't ever see hide or hair of him.'

* * *

Billy-boy and Jake rode quietly into town, keeping to the back streets and out of sight of the townsfolk as much as possible. Having discovered a derelict property, they forced an entry into the rear yard.

'You stay here and keep under cover with the horses,' Jake reasoned as he unbuckled the flap of one of his saddle-bags. 'I'l take this and the letter, find out where the old guy's hangin' out, then do what's necessary.'

'No!' The breed struck his chest noisily with the flat of his hand. 'I go!' Billy-boy bared his teeth and scowled. 'I find out where he stay . . . plenty damn quick.'

Jake merely shifted his plug of tobacco to the other cheek.

'Oh! And then what?'

'I cut his friggin' throat if he don't give plenty money.'

Jake sighed his disgust and looked pityingly at Billy-boy.

'Hey, Billy-boy, ya sure yer momma wasn't joshin' when she told ya . . . yer pa was a white man?'

'Sure. A mountain man. All tribe know that.'

'Well, in that case, why in tarnation can't ya get it through yer thick skull yet?' Jake asked. 'We haven't come here for any friggin' money. That ain't the plan. The boss's after a whole lot more.' It was Jake's turn to bang his chest, emphasizing the point. 'I go. I take the letter and the parcel.'

Minutes later as Jake came to the end of an alley, he struck lucky. On the other side of Main Street, outside a gunsmith's, stood Walter Krank. The old man was making his mouth go, giving out orders to a bunch of men as Jake had seen him do so many times during the winter.

Jake pulled back quickly into the

alley out of sight. Peeping from the corner of the building he wondered how to carry out his mission. He would have to be extra careful. After all, he had not bargained to find the mine owner out in the open and surrounded by his men.

Footsteps approaching along the boardwalk caused the outlaw to duck back again and press himself against the wood-planked wall. A boy, barely in his teens, stepped from the end of the boardwalk and, not noticing him, set off to cross the dusty alley.

'Psst!' Jake hissed, remaining out of sight of the miners. 'Here, boy.'

The youngster half-turned to see who had called, but unimpressed, walked on.

'Wanna earn yourself a dollar?'

The youth pulled up in mid-stride. He turned, squinting one eye in disbelief as he pointed a skinny finger at the centre of his equally skinny chest.

'Ya mean me, mister?' Cautiously he halved the distance between them.

'You're offerin' me a whole dollar?'

'That's right, I can see you're a real smart boy.'

'What ya want I should do?' he asked suspiciously, backing away half a stride. 'I ain't doin' nothin' my pa said I shouldn't. You're a stranger. I won't go inside no livery barn with ya, not even for a dollar, no sir, not even two.'

'You got me all wrong, son.' Jake smiled as sweetly as a priest at collection time. He showed him the small package parcelled up in dirty yellow oilskin, cu' from an old slicker and tied with string. 'All I want ya t' do is deliver this . . . with a letter.' Cautiously he pointed around the corner. 'To that old fella. See him, the one standin' over on the boardwalk, by that gun store?'

The boy frowned, gazed across at Walter, then looked back.

'Why pay me a dollar when all you've got t' do is walk over and stick it in his hands yourself?'

'Hell, son, you sure are mighty suspicious for a Christian, ain't ya?'

'Mister, I know what goes on. I ain't dumb, if that's what ya mean.'

'I know that, boy. Anybody would know ya ain't.' He indicated Walter again. Lowering his voice he explained further. 'Ya see that old man . . . it's his birthday.' He held out the parcel and the boy accepted it dumbly. 'This is a kinda surprise present for him.'

'Oh!' The youth grinned fit to split his face in two, 'I get it.'

Slipping a silver dollar into the grasping hand already held out to him, Jake also passed over the letter and gave his final instructions.

'Now remember, son . . . it's a surprise. I don't want him to know it's me who's givin' this.' He began to sidle back along the alley. 'Give me time to get out of sight before you hand anythin' over. Ya got that?'

'I got it, mister.'

'Count to a hundred . . . real slow.'

'A hundred?' It was a heck of a lot

of counting. Childlike he shifted his weight continuously from one foot to the other, eager to join in the game and wanting to spend his new-found money on candy sticks before Papa could get his hands on it. 'OK, mister, ya can rely on me.'

As soon as the outlaw disappeared around a corner, the lad began.

'One, two, three . . . '

* * *

Walter Krank turned as the youth patted him hesitarily on the back.

'What ya want, kid?'

The boy thrust both the package and the letter into his grasp, then dashed away.

'Happy birthday.' He twisted round and called out, in a voice on the point of breaking. Then before any questions could be asked, his booted feet clattered along the sidewalk and around a corner.

Puzzled, Walter watched the youth

disappear from view, then hefted the package in one hand, mentally weighing it. Suspicious, he frowned, attempting to figure out what it contained and who had sent it.

'Didn't know it was yer birthday, boss,' Dick Hickory remarked, loading a box on to the flat cart. 'Just how old are ya?'

'It ain't my birthday,' Walter murmured. 'And as for my age . . . that, my friend, is my business.'

The fingers of his right hand were already undoing the parcel. A round metal lid was exposed first.

'Mmm, looks like a jar of some sort. Seems one of you guys is playin' some kind of joke. Yeah, it's a jar of pickles. It's . . . ' He gasped and then almost dropped the jar after peering through the glass. 'Jesus Christ . . . it's a pickled ear!'

In no time at all he was surrounded with keenly interested viewers, all peering at the grisly object floating in the jar of cheap whisky.

'Who is it?' a voice asked.

'Who in the hell d'ya think?' Dick hissed. 'It's Solomon's. Anyone can see that. Seems he ain't comin' back.'

Walter Krank's features had turned as white as they would ever be. He swayed and for a second or so looked as though he would pass out. The carpenter pushed past the others, took hold of the jar and passed it to another man.

'Come on, boss, let's you an' me cross the road and sink a couple of shots of whisky, eh?'

Walter said nothing, but allowed the younger man to lead him over to the saloon and sit him in the shaded bar with an opened bottle and a glass.

'I can't believe he's dead . . . not Solo.'

'Know exactly how ya feel, boss. He was built like a tree.' Dick nodded seriously. 'The kind that lives for ever.'

Walter placed his elbow on the table and rested his head on his fist. There was the rustle of paper, reminding him that he still clutched the letter. With shaking fingers he tore open the envelope, smoothed out the single sheet of paper and, watched by an interested Dick Hickory, read the pencilled message.

The carpenter watched life return to the wrinkled face before him. Walter sat up and breathed in deeply, then let out a heavy sigh of relief.

'The bushwhackers say he's alive.' Slapping the table with the palm of his hand, he blurted out, 'Solo . . . he's wounded . . . but he's alive.'

'But that's his ear in the jar. We all know that,' Dick exclaimed.

'But that don't say he's dead, does it?' Stabbing at the pencilled message he went on to explain. 'If I don't do exactly what the gang boss says he wants in this letter . . . in three days' time Solo's gonna lose the other one. And then some different part of'im every day . . . until I settle up.'

After a long period of silence between them, Dick leaned closer and whispered so as not to be overheard by other customers who had come in and now sat at the next table.

'What's he want . . . the outlaw boss, I mean?'

The old-timer sat up and sighed.

'All my money . . . and Solo's, and . . . ' Walter suddenly looked much older than he actually was.

'And? Go on, boss. What else?' his companion pressed gently.

'Wants the papers signed over all legal-like.' He gazed directly at the carpenter. 'Wants me to give him the mine, lock, stock and barrel.' Raising his hands in a gesture of utter hopelessness, he shrugged. 'The bastards . . . they want everythin' Solo an' me's got in the world.'

'What, all you've worked for?' Angered he got to his feet. 'Now don't you worry, boss, we're not sittin' back an' lettin' them varmints get away with it.' He pulled on his cap. 'I'm gonna see me some ladies, round 'em up and get 'em workin' for us.'

'Ladies?' Walter's eyes popped wide open in surprise. 'What in the . . . ' He paused and looked closely at Dick. 'Ya gone addled between the ears? Women ain't no use to us. It's fightin' men we need.'

'You wait an' see, boss,' Dick advised. 'We ain't beaten yet.'

10

Walter had grown bleary-eyed with the booze. Through the cushion of an alcoholic mental fog, it gradually dawned upon him that some kind of commotion was developing outside the saloon. Naturally inquisitive, he left his seat at the bar-room table and ambled unsteadily out through the swing doors. He nudged one of the other interested onlookers already standing on the veranda.

'Hey, what's goin' on out there?' he asked, pushing past to see a swarm of agitated and determined women marching down Main Street. 'Who are they? Where they headin'?'

'Dunno,' grinned the cowhand. 'But them ladies are wearin' their Sunday-best hats. I just know I wouldn't stand in their way. They're all fired up, so it looks like they mean business, wherever it is.'

The procession of women halted outside the most impressive building in town. Breaking ranks, they bunched around the entrance and began to chant loudly in unison.

'What's that place?' Walter asked the same cowboy.

'The mayor's office. Can't ya hear? They're callin' for him to come out.'

Concentrating his full attention, the old-timer cocked an ear and gradually sorted out the words.

'We want the mayor! We want the mayor!' The screeching females continued to chant monotonously. 'We want justice.'

'Come on, fellas. Let's go take a closer look-see, an' have us some fun,' another ranch-hand yelled drunkenly from the far side of the veranda. Laughing and joking most of the crowd went along to watch and listen. 'Come on, boys. Let's help the little ladies. Altogether now . . . we want the mayor! We want the mayor!'

The glass door of the building

189

opened and the town mayor, his hooked thumbs gripped in his jacket lapels, stepped out to confront the noisy horde. Bumptious, standing to his full height of five feet in high-heeled boots, he stuck out his several chins and adopted an imperious stance.

One by one the catcalls and shouts died away, but he did not say a word until the last sound had ceased. At last he smiled, a smarmy 'Vote for me' kind of smile. And when he opened his mouth the words he emitted were automatic, laced with diplomatic balm and goo.

'Ladies. How nice to see such a veritable sea of beauty before me. I must admit it is indeed a rare pleasure for such a busy man as myself.' As if to prove his point he took out his gold hunter from his vest pocket and held it to advantage as he read the time. 'But then, I'm sure all you clever ladies know, I have many difficult and sometimes tedious duties to perform.'

'Bullshit!' yelled a male onlooker

from the back. 'Ya wouldn't recognize duty if it smacked ya in the puss.'

The mayor refused to look towards that challenge. Instead he pretended he had not heard as his fixed smile beamed down on the womenfolk.

'Now . . . ' Rubbing his hands like a miser he swivelled his head left and right, searching. 'Now who's going to be the lucky one to explain what it is I can do for you? Yes, what can it be that you all want me to provide so badly, eh?'

'Justice!' The single word hissed, and wafted through the crowd like a breeze.

The mayor's face crumpled as he frowned.

'Justice? I don't understand.'

'We all guessed ya wouldn't,' joked the same wag who had heckled before. He burst out laughing and everyone around him laughed along with him. His Worship The Mayor joined in too, but could not conceal the anger boiling up within him.

'Mister Mayor,' cried out the widow of one of the murdered miners. 'My man is dead. Murdered by outlaws outside of town and you . . . you've given us a sheriff who don't give a damn.'

'They killed off my man at the same time,' shrieked the other dead miner's wife and I want somethin' done about it.'

'I don't quite understand,' the puzzled mayor began.

'That ain't a surprise. Ya never did. That's yer trouble, fella,' the blacksmith's voice boomed from the back of the crowd. 'If it don't make money for you an' yer pals on the council, ya don't want t' know.'

'Yeah, an' that yella-backed lawman ya sicced on to the town,' bellowed Walter Krank. 'There ain't no way he's aimin' to do a thing about finding them murderin' varmints and bringin' them to justice.'

'And those same outlaws, now they're holdin' another fella to ransom,' Dick

Hickory joined in, keeping the pressure on the mayor. 'They're threatenin't' cut him to pieces, then kill him if they don't get their way.'

'Yeah, so what ya gonna do about it?' the two miners' widows taunted in harmony. 'The same as yer useless office-bound sheriff's done? Nothin'!'

'Ladies . . . ladies, please,' the town's leading citizen pleaded, expressively waving his arms and patting the air with his hands to quieten them down.

'We ain't ladies,' interrupted a skinny hooknosed woman who would have looked more at home riding a broomstick, screeching at him from the front row. 'We're each and every one of us voters' wives.' She shook her fist, nodding her head knowingly. 'Our menfolk are voters . . . d'ya hear that, Mister Mayor?' she asked emphatically.

'And we women know the way to change our men's votes,' one of the younger women added, looking around at those near her, and craftily grinning.

'That right, girls?'

A sea of hats nodded enthusiastically.

'You bet we can.'

'The ladies are right,' Dick butted in once more. 'None of the fellas are gonna like ya bein' the cause of that. Just you chew on that little thought for a while. The next round of town elections'll be a-comin' round in a month or two. And that time'll come an' go mighty fast.'

'If ya know what's good for you, Mister Mayor,' the blacksmith shouted again, 'you'll see to it that the law starts to work around here. Otherwise . . . well, hecky-me, fella, you ain't an idiot. There's no need for anybody t' spell it out for ya, is there?'

* * *

Solomon Jackson took advantage of sleep-time to heal. On this particular morning he woke to discover that apart from the soreness of his bound wrists, his other pains were hardly noticeable.

White Fawn appeared as silently as usual, bringing him some breakfast. She sat carefully on one side of the bed, feeding him.

'You Cradock's woman?' Solo whispered as she leaned close to spoon the food beween his lips.

She glanced fearfully towards the open doorway before whispering back her reply.

'No . . . prisoner, same as you.'

'Can you get a knife for these ropes?'

She tensed and drew back, checking the doorway once again.

'No! They would kill me.'

'Ya got a man?'

She shook her head and shovelled the last of the food into his mouth before he could ask more.

His eyes stared straight into hers and she stared back.

'You be my woman?' he whispered urgently. 'Set me free . . . I'll be good to you.'

Her lips tightened and as she tipped the tin mug against his lower lip her hand was shaking.

'No . . . we would both die.'

'Not if we're careful,' he contradicted after he had gulped the coffee. 'Set me free. I'll make you my wife. You'd have a house . . . a real house . . . clothes. Everything you'd want.'

Again she shook her head, but this time he could tell she was no longer so determined.

'You're a white man!'

'That makes no difference.'

She creased her forehead and considered this last remark as she administered the rest of the coffee.

'No woman warms your bed?'

'No. That's the truth.'

For a fleeting moment her spontaneous smile flashed good white teeth. Then a growl from the direction of the doorway wiped the emotion from her face.

'So! Seems you've got somethin' I ain't, Mountain Man,' Jake pointed out as he clumped over the floorboards with the rowels of his spurs jingling. 'But I wouldn't get yer hopes up . . . she's like a block of ice to white men.'

White Fawn quickly collected the breakfast utensils and attempted to hurry out past the leering outlaw. His hand reached out, grabbed her left breast and squeezed so hard that she gasped with pain.

'Let her be,' Solo threatened.

'Or else?' Jake snarled, relaxing his hold just long enough for the Indian girl to twist free and make a desperate dash from the room. 'What you gonna do about it?'

'Cut me loose an' I'll soon show ya. Ya hunk o' horse shit.'

Jake's right hand blurred as it slapped leather and drew. The hammer clicked back and, in a split second the barrel of his pistol had split Solo's lips, and then it rattled in past his teeth and was held there. Solo lay unable to move or speak, almost choking, his tongue tasting the salt of his blood mixed with the oil which still clung to the cold steel barrel.

Jake's eyes stared, wild and malevolent,

as he looked past his gun-hand.

'Mister, I'll show ya who's horse shit.'

'Pull that trigger, Jake and I'll blow yer friggin' head off yer shoulders.'

The icily delivered words had an immediate calming effect. The foresight of the handgun chipped the edge of a front tooth as it was withdrawn from Solo's mouth, letting him breathe easy once more.

'The big bastard was ridin' me, boss.'

'I don't give a preacher's fart if ya was gettin' raped. Ya mule-headed fool. That guy's big money to us, don't you forget that. And today's supposed to be the big day, ain't it?'

Sheepishly Jake uncocked and holstered his gun as he turned his back on Solo.

'Yeah you're right, boss. The big day. He can wait 'til later when we've got what we want from the old-timer . . . if he shows up accordin' to plan.'

'He'll turn up all right,' Cradock

stated with confidence. 'His kind always does the right thing.' He grinned. 'Besides, didn't you deliver my invitation?'

'Sure did, boss.'

Spitting on the floor, the gang boss sneered.

'Loyalty, they call it.' He looked down at his silent prisoner. 'That's right, ain't it, Mountain Man?' No answer came. He laughed. 'Huh! Loyalty. I ain't seen any of that for one hell of a long time. Certainly not around here.'

'What ya mean, boss?' Jake asked, bewildered.

Cradock merely spat again, and rubbed the spittle into the dust of the floor with the sole of his boot.

'Nothin' . . . Ya wouldn't understand, even if I carved it on yer hide.' His mood had changed. He had come to a decision. 'Right, go tell the boys to saddle up ready. It's time to move out and get into position for the old man.'

When Jake had left the room and could be heard shouting the boss's orders to the rest of the outlaws, Cradock began to gloat.

'Well, big fella, this could turn out t' be your lucky day. In a few hours you could be seein' that old goat of a partner of yours.'

'Ya lettin' me go?'

The outlaw looked pained.

'Please! Do I look stupid? If I win, lose or draw, it'll make no difference t' you . . . or your partner if he comes. You're gonna die . . . you an' him. But that's no real surprise to you, is it?'

'You're wastin' yer time, Cradock. Walt's loyal all right, but he ain't gonna be dumb enough to walk in and hand ya the papers and gold on a plate. As likely as not you'll be findin' a sheriff's posse shootin' holes through y'all.'

Cradock laughed heartily.

'The sheriff?' He went on laughing and slapping his thighs. 'Why d'ya think we made this our hide-out? That's one lawman we need never be afeared of.

He don't ever leave town, not for anythin'. Everyone knows that.'

'Walt won't come.'

'He'd better.'

'Well you're gonna be real disappointed when he don't, ain't ya?' Solo taunted.

'If he don't turn up . . . well, ya should recall what I said after I'd sliced yer ear off. I'll be sendin' him the other one t' make up the pair.' With an evil smirk, he slid Solo's hunting knife from its sheath and began to strop it on his palm. 'I enjoy using this. It's a really good blade.'

★ ★ ★

Hot, thirsty and with his nerves on edge, Walter Krank drove the flat cart at a comfortable pace for the team, following the stage route. Alone and unarmed, as directed in the letter received with Solo's pickled ear, he headed for the rendezvous.

Since having left the town behind,

he had kept his eyes peeled. With each bone-shaking mile he had half expected the outlaws to alter the arrangements, and turn up sooner than anticipated in order to fool any devious plan.

The chances of Solo and himself surviving the remainder of the day were slim. Walter was too long in the tooth to have false illusions on that score. However, he was willing to gamble his own life for that of his friend, go along with the outlaws and give them a chance to prove him wrong.

At odd times during the morning, Walter had taken note of intermittent flashes of light reflecting among the rocks away to his left, high up on the ridge.

'All right fella, I ain't blind,' he muttered grimly, 'I know you're out there, checkin' up on me with that spy-glass. There ain't no need to make me feel like a steer on his way to a barbecue.'

He felt better knowing the plan was

actually under way and he was keeping to time. All his life he had dreamed of being a mine owner and had made it. Made it bigger than most, and here he was, at the time of success, willing to give it all away to save a pal.

'Walter Krank,' he groaned, then grinned wryly. 'Ya know somethin', ya silly old fool? You're plumb loco! Yep, that's it in a word . . . loco.' But he knew he would not have it any other way. After all, he had always been an optimist and was as sure as anyone that there would be another mine. 'Yeah,' he breathed, already picturing it in his mind's eye, 'A bigger, richer mine. One with veins of gold ore a yard thick, waiting for me to discover it. Over the horizon, or maybe just below the next ridge.'

The cart drew abreast the stage-line relay station but he ignored it and drove past. It would not be long before he reached the turning that would take him back into Dead Bear Pass.

When he could just make out the

opening to the pass in the distance, he pulled up the team to give them their nosebags. He still had time to change his mind. If he turned the team around now, he would be safe and no one back in town would blame him. They'd say he was being sensible.

Quarter of an hour later he was in the driving seat again. Kicking off the brake he cracked his whip above the animals' heads.

'Yah, yah.' The cart groaned as it was turned off the road and steered towards the pass.

★ ★ ★

Up on the ridge Cradock and his gang sat waiting as the flat wagon drew closer.

'Come on, messenger boy, come t' Daddy,' the leader muttered, focusing his telescope on the driver.

'How much ya reckon we'll get off the old boy, boss?' Jake asked as he flicked the stub-end of his cigarette at a passing butterfly, almost hitting it.

Cradock twisted round. His eyes narrowed in the sunlight and he scowled at Jake.

'We?' he retorted. 'What ya mean . . . *we?*'

The others in the gang, sensing a drama, stopped talking and concentrated their attention on the boss and Jake.

Jake's face and neck flushed like the wattles on a stag turkey. He glanced at the others, pleading for support, but none came.

'Well?' Cradock pressed, enjoying Jake's obvious discomfort. 'What do ya mean . . . this 'we' business?'

'I . . . I just thought . . . I mean, we're a gang ain't we? We're entitled t' have a fair share of what's goin'.'

'You the ramrod of this here outfit?'

'Ah heck, boss, ya know I ain't.'

'But you'd like t' be. Ya kind of fancy yourself in the saddle givin' out the orders, eh, don't ya?'

The flush intensified and head down, Jake broke into a grin. He rubbed at the sides of his face attempting to suppress the silly smile.

'Well . . . would ya?' Cradock pushed some more.

'Suppose so . . . yeah, why not?'

Cradock stood up and, resting his hand on the butt of his pistol, eyed the other gang members.

'Any of you boys not satisfied with the way I run things . . . eh?' His words held the threat of death. Nobody answered. He spoke again, this time in a more mocking tone. 'All right, who among ya thinks Jake would make a better boss than me?'

This time Billy-boy spoke up.

'Only Jake does, boss.' Then he laughed and the others went along with him. Cradock joined in and turned to the embarrassed man.

'Any time you ain't satisfied, Jake . . . ' He patted his holster. 'All ya got t' do is reach for yer gun.' He stood at the ready, his jacket pushed back. 'That what ya want?'

Jake's colour flowed from his face

again. He took a backward step and shook his head emphatically.

'Hell, no, boss . . . ya know me. I was only havin' a joke.' It was his turn to laugh and right on cue, the others joined him. 'Had ya fooled that time, boss.'

'Hey! Here he comes,' Billy-boy warned. 'The old guy's in range.'

Cradock forgot Jake. Taking up a firing position, he levered a round into the carbine and brought the weapon up on aim.

'Here we go, boys,' he exclaimed.

Then his finger closed on the trigger.

11

The outlaw detailed to watch over Solo until the others returned from the rendezvous, sat balancing a creaking chair on its back legs. Silent, he smoked stinking tobacco in an ancient cherry-wood pipe.

All morning he had waited, a mean-featured, suspicious look on his unshaven face, doing nothing more productive than blowing smoke rings. Scraping out the bowl of his pipe, it came as a surprise to his prisoner when at last, the guard broke the silence.

'You're gonna die,' he mentioned casually to Solo as if remarking on the weather. Pausing, he took great care to shake the accumulated spittle and tobacco juice from the stem. 'But then, yer not dumb, I guess ya already know that, don't ya?'

Solo had already arrived at that

conclusion, but to hear it confirmed by someone else caused his mouth to dry like a sun-bleached skull. His skin crawled as the chilling words chewed further into his mind. But he forced a derisive smile, as though he no longer gave a hoot.

'Everyone has t' die sometime . . . even you.'

Apparently unimpressed, the guard gave the pipe bowl a final scrape with his pocket knife, blew hard through the stem, then began to refill it with coarse black tobacco.

'That's true enough.' His toothless mouth gaped into a grin as he leaned forward and pointed the pipe stem like an extra finger. 'But most folks don't die the way you're gonna. Yes, friend . . . ' He wagged the pipe stem. 'Just wait till the breed gets his paws on ya.'

Solo simply stared at the guard, who laughed, stuffed the pipe in his mouth and struck a match to light the fresh tobacco. Only after the third match had done the job, did he condescend to speak again.

'I tell ya this much, you ain't seen anythin' like it. That Billy-boy, he's a real artist when it comes t' torture.' Breaking off, he seemed to let his mind drift into thought for a while. Finally he shook his head. 'Nope, I ain't able t' bring t' mind any man who enjoys hurtin' folks so much. Not even a full-blooded Sioux Indian, and believe me, friend, I've been around and watched a few in my time.'

'You're a regular Daddy Christmas, all heart, ain't ya?' Solo scoffed, bluffing to conceal his fears. 'You're just tryin' t' cheer me up.'

White Fawn, calling from the doorway, interrupted them.

'You want I should bring coffee?'

'Yeah, and make it quick,' the guard snarled back. 'I'm parched close t' chokin' t' death.' Impulsively he stood and stretched, grinning down at Solo. 'What ya think of the little squaw? Ain't she a dandy filly?' He winked suggestively. 'Bet you'd sooner be hangin' out of her, than from the edge of a cliff.'

Solo glared back, his mouth twisted in disgust.

'You're filth, ya know that?' Solo spat the words, but they made no impression. The guard merely laughed.

'Yeah, that's me. I'm filth all right, but mister, at the end of t'day I'll be live filth. That's more than you'll be.' Then he sneered. 'Buzzard meat!'

From the corner of his eye, Solo was aware of the Indian girl again. Her hands supported a tin tray on which balanced an open-topped coffee jug and a tin mug. She made a bee-line for the guard.

'Don't hand it to me, woman, I don't want t' hold the damn thing,' the outlaw remonstrated, displaying his deep-seated loathing for her race. 'Put it yonder on the table, ya heathen bitch, and then pour the friggin' stuff into a cup like a civilized woman would.'

White Fawn did neither. As if deaf to his orders, she ignored him and advanced, then suddenly hurled the tray and its steaming contents into his face.

As hot black coffee drenched the surprised guard's face and chest, he swore, and squealed as loudly as a frightened pig. Frantically, he pawed at his eyes, attempting to disperse the scalding fluid.

But his inflicted pain lasted only for a second or so. White Fawn, brandishing the knife she had concealed in her hand beneath the tray, darted in close to the outlaw. Choosing a spot, she lunged, burying the slender blade deep into his ribs.

The pathetic screaming stopped at once. The guard stared at her in goggle-eyed disbelief, coughing painfully as his fingers clawed at the hilt of the knife. Bright frothing blood belched from his mouth, as he attempted to step towards her. Twisting as his knees sagged, he fell back and landed heavily on the floor.

With a noisy rattle from the back of his throat, his final breath gurgled out.

Ignoring the stickiness of the blood-covered handle, White Fawn knelt and withdrew the knife from the dead man's chest. Without bothering to clean the blade, she quickly sawed and slashed through the ropes binding Solo to the bed.

'You keep promise, like you say?' she asked.

Solo struggled to sit up. Cramped and stiff he rubbed his wrists hard to restore the circulation. For a moment his eyes met hers. He frowned at her natural female distrust.

'Lady,' he growled, 'if I make a promise, to anyone, I keep it . . . no matter what!'

Her tenseness left her and with a smile of delight flashing across her fine smooth features, she nodded her satisfaction.

'White Fawn make fine wife.'

★ ★ ★

The team leader tumbled and fell under the hoofs of its partner, bringing it down too. At that same moment, Walter Krank heard the single shot from the carbine on the ridge away to his left.

'Whoa there . . . whoa!' he yelled angrily. 'Steady now, steady, damn yer hides.' Hauling hard on the reins, wrestling and cursing, he managed to control the bucking of the two startled animals remaining on their feet. Pulling on the handbrake at the side of the driving seat he looped the reins round it and held up his hands.

As the tripped horse finally scrambled to its feet again, Walter, still keeping his hands high and in full view, slowly stepped down and stood, waiting.

'Hey, old-timer!'

Owing to the echoes, and the fact that he was now squinting almost directly into the sun, the origin of the shout was impossible for Walter to locate.

'Yeah . . . what ya want?'

'Ya bring the papers for the mine?'

'Yeah . . . that's why I'm here, ain't it? Ya brought my partner?'

'Ya got the gold?' the voice continued, avoiding the question.

'What's left of it. Where's my partner?'

'Ya signed them papers like you're supposed to?'

'Not until I see my partner's OK, I won't.'

Whoever had been shouting, stopped for a time. When he resumed his manner seemed more reasonable and relaxed.

'OK, fella, we'll take ya to see him. You can drop your hands, but no funny stuff. Leave the wagon and walk on into the pass until I tell ya t' stop. Go on, get movin'.'

Setting off as if out for a Sunday walk, Walter strolled along the pass. Thrusting his hands into his pockets he permitted himself a smile of anticipation.

Pushing his fingers through a pocketful of loose glass trade-beads, he forced an opening between the stitching of the pocket lining then pushed a bead through the newly made hole. With satisfaction he felt the bead fall down inside his trouser leg, rattle on to his boot, and bounce off to lie on the ground only half a pace away. There, the cheap glass winked in the sunlight like a precious stone, a ruby resting in the dust.

'That's number one,' Walter muttered. 'Hope this's gonna work.' Keeping his eyes on the trail ahead, his rough-skinned fingers manoeuvred the next bead and prepared to evict one every few yards.

★ ★ ★

'This fella . . . he the only one left here?' Solo asked White Fawn as he swiftly removed the gunbelt from the dead outlaw and buckled it around his own narrow waist.

'Yes, we are alone.'

'Have ya noticed a white mule around here? Real big, with black eyes.'

'In the cave,' she boasted, eager to please. 'I've watered and fed it well since that half-breed, Billy-boy brought him in, about an hour after you arrived here.'

Nelly nuzzled affectionately in response to a few energetic pats on her neck, while Solo looked around for his saddle.

'What's happened to the saddle she was wearin'? Ya know?'

'Cradock wanted it. Gave his old one to Billy-boy.' The squaw led him to a straw-filled corner of the cave and dragged out an old beaten-up cavalry saddle. 'This was Billy-boy's.' Panting, she hefted another, a Texas saddle. 'This is dead man's.'

Having helped her into the saddle of the dead guard's horse, Solo swung himself into Nelly's temporary saddle.

'Which direction did Cradock and his boys take? Did ya hear anythin' said?'

'Dead Bear Pass,' the Indian girl answered as they set off to ride out of the cave. 'The sunrise end, the way your friend told to come.'

'Hmm, it figures,' he remarked thoughtfully, more to himself than her. 'It's the safest place for 'em. From there they can see for miles, checkin' if a posse or anybody's comin' up behind.'

'What we do now?'

His gaze made no secret of her attraction for him. But he quickly dragged himself back to the reality of the present.

'You do nothin'. But me . . . I'm gonna save old Walt's hide.'

'I come with you.'

'No! You stay out of it.'

'Me come with you.' With the skill of a magician, her hand slipped inside her buckskins, producing the same knife she had used to kill the guard. 'Me your woman. Kill all enemies.'

Solo could not help but smile.

'Hey, I haven't got all that many enemies.'

'Me follow.'

He drew his gun and pointed it at her horse's head.

'That critter you're ridin', I can easily shoot it.'

'Then I walk,' she persisted. Smiling sweetly, she pleaded. 'Me go . . . yes?'

Her smile forced him to grin.

'OK, put that knife away. You can come along,' he agreed stern-voiced. 'But you'll have t' do as you're told.'

'All time,' she agreed innocently. 'Me good woman. No need to beat me . . . much.'

★ ★ ★

Having hidden inside the relay station since the night before, the sheriff and his posse kicked their heels in boredom. From behind shuttered windows they had seen the old mine owner drive past, and turn his wagon off for Dead Bear Pass. A while later a single distant gunshot told them the action had really begun.

'Blast the mayor,' the sheriff grumbled.

'Him and his no-account voters. Why in hell didn't he come along himself if he was s' damned keen?'

'Reckon it's time to go yet, Sheriff?' one of his gun-happy deputies asked for the third time in about as many minutes.

'What's wrong with ya, boy? Wanna get yourself shot full o' holes an' buried before yer time?'

'We've gotta let 'em ride clear of the area before we follow,' Dick Hickory explained to the deputy. 'It won't be long now.'

Checking his pocket watch, the unenthusiastic sheriff replaced it carefully. Groaning a sigh, he jerked his head at the door. 'Saddle-up. We'll soon know if the rest of the old fool's idea works out or not.'

Beneath the relentless blazing sun, the three living horses of the wagon team stood forlornly, effectively anchored beside their dead companion, but there was no blood on the driving seat and the cantankerous old-timer's body was nowhere around.

'Well, seems he got that part right. They ain't killed 'im yet, but they've taken him with 'em.' The senior lawman mopped the sweat from his flaccid face. He waved an arm. 'Dismount. Spread out and look around for them beads of his.' Then, remaining in the saddle, he mumbled, 'Huh, beads . . . what a damned stupid notion.'

'Here, Sheriff,' came the almost immediate and excited yell from the action-keen deputy. He stood in the middle of the trail, some twenty yards further on. 'It's a glass bead.' He held it up between finger and thumb. 'A red one . . . look.'

'I've seen beads before,' the impatient sheriff snarled. 'Well, what ya waitin' for? Move along. Follow 'em!' Walking his horse, he added, 'And who knows, maybe you'll find enough t' make yourself a sweet little necklace just like the other gals.'

★ ★ ★

From the cave mouth, Solo and White Fawn were startled to see the gang already herding their latest prisoner on foot towards the hide-out.

'Back!' Solo urged, desperately reining Nelly so that she spun nimbly round and returned to the gloom of the cave again. White Fawn was only a fraction slower, but he had already slipped from the saddle and gripped the six-gun by the time she was under cover. Each breathed sighs of relief as no shots rang out.

'That's done it. Just my luck. They've got Walt, and now we're boxed in good and tight again,' Solo groaned.

'Men bring horses in here soon,' she whispered. Withdrawing her knife, she peeped over his shoulder as he crouched close to the cave entrance watching those outside.

'That'll be fun,' he commented dryly.

Her free hand gently stroked his cheek.

'We fight . . . die together. Yes?'

12

'In ya go, mister,' demanded a jubilant Cradock, passing the reins of his mount to one of his henchmen. 'Go an' say hello to yer partner.'

Grimly, Walter pursed his lips, expecting the worst as he stepped inside the cabin.

'Go on . . . straight ahead,' urged the gang boss from outside. 'That mountain man's a lazy dog, always busy sleepin' at this time of day.' Cradock laughed.

Through the doorway to another room, Walt made out an empty bed. He approached cautiously, then stopped. On the floor, poking out from the other side of the bed were the booted feet of a man. The toes pointed at the roof and had a stillness about them which told a familiar story.

'Holy Moses!' He stared at the

cadaver. In a wave of relief he sat on the creaking bed and dared to breathe again. 'Thank the Lord. It ain't him.'

Shortly after, heavy footsteps followed him and stopped by the foot of the bed.

'What in the name of . . . ?' Cradock eyed the dead man only for an instant. Unperturbed by the corpse, he appeared far more concerned in looking around the rest of the room in a panic. 'Where is he?' His voice rose in sudden rage, betraying a touch of hysteria. 'Where is he?'

Encouraged by this sudden turn in events, Walter Krank grinned, and remained seated with his arms folded. He laughed outright.

'Shut up!' Cradock warned.

'Ha!' Walter exclaimed. 'I didn't reckon a slimy maggot like you could hold Solo Jackson for long. Not if he was still alive an' kickin'.'

Cradock's temper exploded. Whipping out his pistol he side-swiped the old-timer with a single vicious blow, knocking him off the bed to tumble unconscious on top of the corpse. Then without a second thought for his victim, the outlaw boss dashed out of the room in a rage.

'The mountain man,' he yelled. 'The big bastard's escaped . . . and so's that Indian whore. What ya waitin' for? Find 'em both . . . Now!'

'Where the friggin' hell was Hank, while they were makin' a getaway?' Jake grumbled in disbelief.

'Well, it ain't no use ya askin' me or Hank,' Cradock yelled at him. 'I wasn't here, and Hank, he's deader than last year's dried fish.'

'That squaw. It was her, the cold-arsed bitch.' Jake's lips curled down with hate. 'It must've been the squaw. There ain't no other way.'

Inside the cave Solo and White Fawn, working at top speed, unsaddled the horse and mule before returning both animals to their makeshift stalls. Then, having little choice, they hid themselves in the darkest corner among sacks of feed and jumbled piles of miscellaneous stores.

That was when the commotion began outside.

'Seems they've discovered that the body's there, but we ain't,' Solo whispered. She snuggled closer and laid her head against his shoulder.

'You think Sioux woman make good wife?' she murmured softly. 'Good, like white woman, maybe?'

'Don't ya think of anythin' else?' As his words died he crushed her fiercely to him, and kissed her hard.

'Good, like a white woman,' he repeated. 'No, not good,' he gasped. 'For me . . . better!'

A distant jingle of spurs interrupted the moment. Two figures appeared, silhouetted at the entrance. Together they took tentative steps from the sunlight into the comparative darkness of the cavern.

'They ain't in here, Billy-boy,' one said, his words echoing. 'Think about it. They'd have saddled up, taken the horses an' high-tailed it. They're on foot out there, let's go. We'll run 'em down in no time at all.'

As the breed ignored him, the speaker spun angrily on his heel.

'Aw, suit yerself, fella!' Bow-legged, he marched out to continue the search elsewhere.

But the half-breed advanced slowly with his gun held waist-high, ready. Step by step, his head twisting frequently, he looked this way and that, ears cocked for the slightest alien noise.

Solo's fingers tapped softly at White Fawn's wrist then slid along to take the knife from her hand. Armed for silent combat, he waited.

Methodically the breed inspected every stall and shadow. With no sound, except for the occasional jingle of his spurs, he drew nearer to the feed sacks.

Billy-boy was close enough now for the fugitives to smell his sweat and hear his breathing. Through a narrow gap between two full sacks, Solo noticed the scuffed toe-caps of their hunter's cowboy boots as they came into view.

Like arrows, the boots pointed to where Solo crouched. As they moved closer, the mountain man's muscles tensed like a drawn bow. He felt the sack move as the breed leaned over it. Then Billy-boy was gawping down at him, face to face.

* * *

Walter regained consciousness. Already his right eye had swollen and was almost closed by the pistol whipping. Weakly he dragged himself off the dead outlaw and, head in hands, sat on the bedstead taking in deep breaths while he pulled himself round some more.

The cabin was silent but there was plenty of action outside. A twinge of memory caused him to feel inside the back pocket of his pants then sigh in relief.

Ducking below window level, he hurriedly searched for any weapon which had been overlooked. He found one, Solo's converted flintlock pistol, but without powder horn or minie balls. Checking, he discovered a percussion cap still on the nipple. Probing the barrel with the ramrod he could tell a charge was still in place and ready wadded, but no ball.

After only a moment's thought, he emptied the remaining glass beads from his pocket into the barrel and wadded them down tight with a strip torn from his shirt-sleeve.

Walter cocked the Kentucky pistol and took up a position at the table, facing the door. He removed the glass funnel from the oil lamp and lit the wick.

'Right-oh, ya bushwhackin' coyote, I'm ready.' From his back pocket he produced two sticks of dynamite he had brought from town. Each was already capped and fitted with a short fuse. Laying them on the table between himself and the burning lamp, he whispered, 'When old Walt Krank

promises t' blow a man's balls off
. . . that's just what he does.'

* * *

As the breed's pistol came into view,
Solo swept the knife upwards and
outwards in a powerful scything stroke.
He struck so forcibly that he hardly
felt the impact. The blade pierced the
side of Billy-boy's neck then continued
across his throat, severing the artery
and the windpipe without pause on its
way out.

White Fawn cried out as a fountain
of blood sprayed over her and Solo,
drenching both in seconds, while Billy-
boy vainly attempted to stem the flow
with his hands. The revolver fired
harmlessly, the bullet burying itself
deep inside a corn sack, then the
weapon slipped from the breed's grip
and fell with a dull thud at Solo's
feet.

In the darkness they saw the whites
of the half-breed's eyes bulge as he

staggered a few short steps, until his life ran out along with his gore. His body fell against a corn sack then rolled off on to the ground.

'They're in there,' someone outside yelled, and in no time at all it seemed every gun in the whole of creation was firing blindly into the cave.

Solo and the Indian girl could do nothing except hug the ground behind the piled up stores. Bullets whizzed and smacked into boxes. Pickle jars were shattered and corn ran from holed sacks in miniature rivers, while the animals in the stall whinnied and kicked out in fear.

After the first onslaught had died down, Solo fired at Jake, who for once pushed his luck too far, and showed himself for only a second. But that was long enough for the man used to winning at turkey shoots. Jake was dead.

'Hold it,' Solo heard Cradock bawl. The firing ceased. Cradock yelled again. 'Hey, in the cave . . . mountain man?'

'I hear ya.'

'I've got a pal of yours out here. Ya can save his life if ya want. Just walk out with your hands in the air.'

'Drop dead. You come in here.'

'I might do that. Yeah, your partner can walk in ahead of me. He'll make a real dandy shield.'

★ ★ ★

Walter levelled the outdated Kentucky hand-gun as soon as the cabin door swung open.

Cradock realized too late that he had been a fool. He had his own pistol drawn when the old Kentucky belched smoke, peppering his head with glass trade beads. The force hammered him back against the doorpost where he slid down, legs astride and with his pulped face drooping on to his chest.

Placing the empty pistol on the table, Walter lit the fuses of the dynamite sticks. With intense satisfaction, he grimly crossed over and stuck one firmly into the dead man's crotch.

'Fella, you're goin' up in the world.' Then with the fuse of the second dynamite stick rapidly spluttering shorter, he stepped out into the daylight.

The outlaws stood dumbly seeing Walter emerge on his own. Casually he hurled the dynamite among them, forcing everyone to run for their lives.

Sprightly for his age, the old-timer sprinted and dived for cover behind a horsetrough. When the explosions occurred, the cabin disintegrated, its splintered logs and planks flying everywhere. Simultaneously, the stick which exploded in the open covered the whole area in a cloud of choking dust which obscured everything around the cave mouth.

'Don't shoot, Solo! It's me, Walt,' the old-timer yelled into the cave mouth. 'I'm comin' in out of the way.'

'Out of the way?' the mountain man gasped, shaking his hand and pulling him behind cover. 'What ya mean . . . out of the way? We're trapped.'

'There's gonna be a whole heap o' trouble. There'll be shootin' an' killin', an' stuff like that, out there. Listen.'

Outside, a drumming of hoofs shook the ground like a cavalry charge, and a storm of shots rent the air.

'That'll be the sheriff and his posse, along with Dick Hickory and the boys,' Walter gloated triumphantly.

White Fawn moved out from the shadows. The old-timer raised his eyebrows.

'Well, who's this little lady?'

'Seems I've teamed up with another partner.' The man from Kentucky chuckled. 'Meet the wife.'

THE END